Message From
A Native Son From A Cell

The Survivor of Childhood Torture

Julian Martin

ISBN: 978-1-4669-1325-7 (sc)
ISBN: 978-1-4669-1326-4 (e)

Trafford rev. 03/16/2012

 www.trafford.com

North America & international
toll-free: 1 888 232 4444 (USA & Canada)
phone: 250 383 6864 ♦ fax: 812 355 4082

INTRODUCTION

AMERICA'S NATIVE SON'S CRY FROM THE HOLE/CELL/ PRISON Hello, people, I'm the real true American Idiot who broke down right in front of you and with bleachers set up, tickets being sold, and I'm sure some profit being made. The place that this happened at was surrounded by a rebellious crowd of itinerantly almost unemployable sort, so they have to make money somehow. I developed a love hate regard for these surrounding neighbors in the same way that they did.

The fact of the matter is that I'm a Tourette Syndrome victim from all of a lifetime of this child torture with criminal negligence & ultra severe mal-nutrition, the kind where the stomach became distended & trust me, not from being full. The result of this severe starvation which is making the stomach distend is the intestines are consuming themselves.

Now's when I have to strive not to repel any readers of a real true life horror story but basically the just described in-tro. is primarily what this story is about. I really was never acknowledged by this family as formally having any kind of disease, but I was only to be regarded as a nuisance even though I had gone thru all of their abuses and torture/starvations that nearly took my life. It's still hard to write this true account when I've realized that the only way or reason that it will, I know become famous is because of these torrid experiences of mine. Just the same, please don't be repelled, but just read on with wide eyes as now, you are about to be amazed at the extent that a child that was your native son can be made to have to survive in a way that would actually be a game to the parent in charge.

This is the story of the real true American Idiot who knows better than to accuse Green day of stealing my disgruntled look.

This cool look I can cultivate very easily simply by putting on a little eye liner and concealer and probably then smudge it a little which makes you then look like a zombie or someone who is very cute but also very mental, after all, I am a man. There's a little set up for readers required so that you won't become confused as one reads this.

Firstly one needs to know that this book is really two books that you are reading, sort of like reading a book within a book. This story isn't only about my successes and my failures, but it's also about a sinister group of groups who stalk me in my vehicle, anywhere I go or visit or live simply because it seems that I have purchased properties that were occupied by most of the hate groups that you can think of and for now will go without mentioning. Please know also that if I am successful at writing this book with basically only one person assisting me by way of. proofreading this before submission, then this should signify leastwise, that yet again, this may be one of the most successful pieces of art & would thoroughly prove to me without a doubt that I have accomplished greatness once again in my life! I did attend college and learned to write and type etc. but though my skills may be rusty, I am still going to go forward in doing this completely by myself, never mind the hate mongers who are reading this and rebelling as I write every line.

The reasoning by the aggravated creatures stalking me along with my torture mother's reasoning for torturing a toddler in a crib:

"I wanna wait till he writes his book," this is what I'm currently having to put up with, "I can only assume that this means that that is when these cretin repulsive will stop with their terrible harassment. It also could mean that this is when these creeps are going to come up with a real money offer to buy this significant piece of real estate I own they think they own, but I know better as I'm the only one who has ever paid the taxes on this and I also know that the deed is in my name. Notwithstanding how stupid these racists think I am, currently I already have two offers, so I don't even care if it's these racists stalkers, & by the way, this could show just cause in the future of their having raided my properties just so they could get it into their hands. The creepy voices next door, "I'm still proud I got his site (Probably my little trailer park that is much the subject of this book) only my life savings! But boy, I hope these KKK, claiming thru the Raiders are sure they want to claim (my) property!

Again, my book is going to be written as if it were a book w/in a book & is going to be depicting the ratings & ongoing torture/heckling being visited on me by some group of psycho's who are hold up in the apartment next door & they speak exactly the same way the crazies did at my house, my former house that was next to my very small trailer park and now they have been here doing the same taunting for at least 7yrs. It's took them that long to even get an offer to buy the property too!

This absurd taunting of theirs is also & exactly why I moved out of this gorgeous house by my Camelot like trailer park. Especially don't think I didn't know that these racists took this as a signal to thoroughly raid this small adorable neighborhood. I definitely knew that it would be just a matter of time before these lowest elements of the South would take their course so I hope that these people are thru now & we'll see just who becomes the new owners of this sweet little piece of land complete with an ancient dry crick bed and 6 story grandfather oaks from which Spanish Moss hangs so beautifully, I think this is one of the most gorgeous spots on that road for 30 mi's.

Submitted for your approval are some of the taunts that these hate mongers hurl as I write this book; "F'n Mohicans fagot, Sancha's Devilla's son's fagot, "Let's smoke him out, as they know that cigarette smoke irritates me, now at this time I have to interject very critical statements made by these groups about my bui's partner's ownership of the mentioned property. "We have to find a patsy then I was told that one had been found by their groups." The mostly felons & regular jail birds & racists are also occupied in the immediate area of this little burg I manage, these same-ones declaring that their many stays in jail have connected them up even more so that they could carry out such things as ruining me. These same imbeciles told me with their own words, that this was where they'd (racists) have their important meeti'ns. There, they'd plot their plans while in their many stints in jail, so crimes here in this Southern state can still actually be getting planned right in jail & I wouldn't even doubt that such things as cell phones are used, maybe hits arrangements solicited for in jail, as their new edict is to go after gays and Mexicans, & I proudly rep. both groups.

You are aware as an American such things as crimes deliberated right from the institutions such as correction facilities that these creeps are mostly in are filled with their Racist comrades so that such crimes as Raiding my properties, putting hits out on someone are ongoing and these are becoming ideal meeting places for these forever thorns in our sides as Americans, HIDEOUS RACISM!

Going back to "let's smoke him out", So I have to put my air cleaner on high & a surgical mask on to breathe better, so what OK, this won't impede me from completing this book. These I consider one of these creatures weaker tactics, I don't want to bore the readers, but this group of thugs are forever proclaiming we're Raiders, this is what we do & Nazi's & Arian's too* I know we already know this, but, this element is so a predominant integral part of this sad sad story, but it's not my place to be apologizing for this. so, this group are not only probably going to be the very ones that purchase this property of mine, but they are making sounds such as next door has been the Raiders stake out for probably the sole purpose of obtaining my property and trying their hardest to completely ruin me, ha ha. Lets as a public who reads this book decide exactly who the thugs are that think I will let go of my life savings to hate groups so easily. One's bragging that he's broken down to a level of having to learn to type with the idea in his head that in this way I can be defeated. Look I say to such an idiot, knock yourself out, but all one needs to do is simply type up an offer of cash and suddenly I'll be defeated. The main method of drumming up capital as they don't have their own due to wine, women, and song, is to find others, I hope others take this nibble too.

At about the time I started writing this book, the mood towards gay men in this state is as such that an alleged murderer of a gay man ought to get away with it, his last name is Demulio & he also injured a friend of the gay man. Next to follow in this God forsaken state is a trial to acquit an adult for murdering her own child, and she is acquitted much to my anger too as I am a living example of a child who survived tortures that a 1 or 2 yr. old should not have even survived. Now hecklers in adjacent bldg actually just said there goes my Demulio, any in-sight here?" And guess what & by the way, I'm very gay & that's also why I'm going thru with writing basically this horror story based on a real; true story.

While reading this auto-bio based tale, it's of utmost importance that one realizes that I'm all over the abuses & stark horror's of my childhood/adolescence but I have to write this actual account so that once & for all, my abusers are identified & for me any way, my good soul is exonerated. I basically/have been victimized from criminal negligence to held in a cellar (caged & starved with only already scavenged bones (probably by my brothers and sisters all older than myself thrown down at me & trust me, there was never any meat on them, so I learned to survive on the meager cartilage that might be on these bones. At times these bones were sharp so my mom knowing this would try to hit me with them like it was some kind of sport to her this torture & bio' mother. I only got a few nicks from her aim, but I know for a fact I got her square on one (occasion & I think this made her : stop as she now knew that I was going to fight back as I knew all of this was totally wrong.

So the readers know how bad I had it, at 2 1/2, this was a dirt floor crawl space beneath an old Brick school house that my parents had converted to a livable house, & this crawl space beneath our bath at back of the house was meant only for plumbers to install indoor plumbing, it wasn't even high or tall enough for my little 2 yr. old body to I stand up, so I used to get cramped allot & there was absolutely no light so when she'd come to give me the water she'd bring once a day, my eyes would hurt as the light was too bright. Sometimes the bones would hit the dirt, often she'd do this on purpose to see if I could be smart enough to catch or intercept them, so when I wouldn't & they'd hit the ground I'd complain, "I can't even eat that bone you horrible monster, so she'd laugh and say "well I guess that is now your problem isn't it? This is when I had to decide to not be hit by these gnawed bones & or have more injuries or try to catch so I at least could gnaw the cartilage off! Mom also liked to pipe in such comments as "You see how healthy & plump your brothers and sisters are, & you could be just as plump and full as they are if you had just complied and done what I had asked of you," which was something that had made them all sick. The thing I refused to do was to eat human feces. Later this mom would use this act on my siblings by saying a comment like, "You all know that I'm the God in this house and if I say you eat shit, you did but I did not eat feces but Julian didn't eat this & you all see what he got!*' Don't forget I was 2 1/2 yr. old & in that pit for I estimate 4 to 6 months, but at least I was visited regularly so I could go to the bathroom & get my glass of waters Although this may sound incredible to readers, trust me, I wouldn't even want to think up such a repulsive, and nauseating idea.

Also I could go to the bathroom once a day when I got the water then I would be ordered to get back in with a belt or club in her clutch.

You can skip this paragraph if you want as I'm changing the subject and time to now, but, I just came from my beautiful antique trailer house

55 yrs. old & this sinister acquisitive mobile home enterprise that has already acquired my double roof other antique mobile has placed a lock on this prize of mine. Now I have to point fingers as the Raiders are also claiming responsibility for this lowly deed, & they are doing this by way of their set up right next door here where I live, they do this type of stuff anywhere I go, constantly heckling/taunting because I had a terrible propensity to avenge this mother and terrible childhood! I've also heard the voice of the person that operated the park where this home is situated also claim that the co. that they represent are happy to fund such a Raid on me as they are totally Red Neck so they were on these criminal's side that are illegally raiding me, couldn't you guess why?

While reading this acct. please keep in mind how a severity of a rebellious/response will be apt to match or surpass the severity of the abuse of a helpless totally dependent & innocent infant; cracked skull, distended stomach starvation (like Biafra) inserting long sewing needles above my left ear but I managed to stop her before she rotated it when she had already stuck this right into my skull! "Hey, what are you trying to do to me? Still, every morning I have to see the scar that I sustained from this torture mother to my skull with a meat cleaver," & it usually gives me goose bumps because I know much of the world couldn't even have a clue as to how somebody's world & life could get so completely out of whack & in just such a very specific way. I shudder that I haven't been able to (yet capable) of putting this terrible story down on paper, but I just keep having to look at a bunch of puzzled perplexed people that are very angry faces who don't know 1/10 of the morbidness that in the form of delayed stress syndrome flashbacks that usually were most intense during a full moon may cause one to wig out! Maybe this could be the result of partially growing up in a cell *&* only being allowed to have water as your only liquid, injuries to my brain via needles and don't forget the meat cleaver, I'll show anybody the scar that I have trouble covering up on my head.

Every time I comb my hair in the morning I have to see this, and it always pisses me off, so after this book is published & has made some money, I'll have hair transplants putin so seeing this at first of the day doesn't start out my day wrong. This would be what I would come to know as my silent insanity brought on by all of the crimes of the American world that can come to a head and drive a native son to the brink of insanity.

Perhaps after I've written this book, not I, but maybe my torturers, criminal neglectors, taunter's & heckler's and abusers will be the ones regarded in a terrible light instead of me. Somehow, I almost doubt that they will. Now there will be egg on their faces & Baby Jane Hudson's blank glazed eyes should be these culprits punishment. in the end these wrenched memories do not ruin my life because I resolve to make myself strong and even stronger than this abusive mother who tried to kill me on more than one separate occasion.

I SAID MY MOTHER TRIED TO KILL ME, & I didn't make any mistake in declaring this & this mother is now deceased but that is when I've decided to write this account. Also my dad is gone too which is another reason that I didn't quite want to tell about this story in the event that someone might read this to him, as you know, the man went to his grave illiterate. Although his basic only crime as an involved parent was to be gone during the entire time of what I call my childhood imprisonment probably because he was out womanizing, tying on a drunk, or just working or gambling, all of which made this mother mad as hell, mad enough to abuse her children, the children of this man who wasn't there to help with all of us 5 children, imagine that! Perhaps this was the dysfunction of my family that lead to the dungeon type abuse that would visit me at the ripe old age of 2. I'll go one further and admit that these ultra severe abuses would visit me for the rest of my life. Would you think that disclosing such torrid information to a general public would also be mortifying due to the fact that I actually allowed a totally crazy girl who was supposed to be your mother tear you down like this, it's tantamount to admitting defeat by a female to me her son. This is how I regard it, I was made to have to start as if from a new born state on various occasions as these severe abuses caused me to go in to shock on various times. To a point, I regard this as a castration and sub-human treatment including the added abuse of this being done to a helpless child by the very one who's supposed to watch out for me in every way, the way she started out to in the first place.

As for my siblings who were all older than me & them never having come to my rescue, their only other little brother, I can defend them by saying, "had they done anything to defy her and attempted to help me, they would have got what I was getting. As much as I would like to place blame on anyone but me, they were all under the age of 9 too, and she had them terrified too. These siblings of mine who still are alive were as much victims as I was too of a religious zea lot mother much like Ed Geens, the famous mutilator of women that Leather-face of the famous Halloween tales horror movies, yes my mom was a terrific bible thumper.

I a very tiny tyke would find out in time that I was going to have to learn to discern between when I was still regarded as the only other boy, & or how I was a threat to my little sisters, all older than me probably because I had a penis & I was also alive and feeling like a boy a thing that my mother found more troublesome as I began to discover how I was different than the sisters who mostly I was around as my brother took to the outdoors as he grew up, also he liked to hunt with my dad who was a master hunter. I was left alone all the time with girls, girls, girls, did I say girls yet?

Anyway; by the end of this book you are going to see that I have decided not to spend the rest of my life feeling like a little boy who lost the love of his most loved mother forever & always reaching for the impossible forever trying to re-gain a torture mother's love when after she switched channels on most of us kids, she only wanted to be the torture mother of her torture children. Wait till you hear how this mother can brag of how she is able to administer torture to her other torture girlfriends as she would refer to them, she actually bragged to me that she was a member of such a club that had refined methods of torture!

Upon one occasion, I heard my mother brag to her girlfriends torture club that I was her boy torture child, & the way she put it was like she hated males, COULD MOTHER HAVE BEEN THE CREATURE LESBIAN WHO EVEN HATED HER OWN SON BECAUSE HE WAS A MALE? I don't know what mom meant when she told me on several occasions that she was denied membership to an exclusive club only for women simply because she had me and I looked like I was going to be a little queer, what a thing to tell your child & I consider this kind of thing to say as severe child abuse too. While bragging to so called torture club girlfriends, sometimes within earshot, & her girlfriends listening intently these malfeasant friends of hers would then look at me & laugh, when I was all of 5 to 6 yrs. old, she'd say things like, "he's a little sissy, hotito you see, they would cluck a little then have another big raucous laugh 1 guess all at the cost of a little 6 & 7 yr. old child & of course this was my public humiliation just another form of these old hen's torture & humiliation, how absurd their memories seem to me now! Some friends of some mother, & this one had to be mine.

I developed OCD as a result of when I was confined in the dirt floor crawl space at the Brick school house, you could compare this to a parakeet in a cage pacing left and right back and forth, or a mouse running round & round in that little squirrel cage that goes round and round ad infinitum abnauseum!

Although I could not pace back and forth because as you could imagine there wasn't even enough room to stand up much less to pace back and forth, however (sin embargo) there was—enough room to rock back and forth. Now then I discovered that I might be able to play with the ants that were crawling around me, probably because they could smell the bones that I would throw on the dirt floor after I would gnaw off the cartilage, I still like to do this as I from the age of 2^ would develop a taste for cartilage as this would be the only food I would ever get to eat during this toddler incarceration. I was just a little boy that was so bewildered remember, so I really didn't know how to survive this, but I eventually would & one of the ways was to try to incorporate these ants as my little friends, but as I contemplated this, I would decide instead to torture these ants the very way that my imprisonment was torturing me. I say that this was torturing me because I everyday had to hear my other brothers" and sisters playing up above with their full stomachs, while I continued to emaciate in. the crawl space below, now how do you think that a 2 year old could figure out how to survive in such a predicament? First I tried to trap these much the way my mother had me trapped in this tiny space, then sometimes these bones would be the only toys I would know, so I'd gloat back to my mother that I did have some toys, & I would tell her that she wasn't going to win & sometime she was going to be discovered. I thoroughly knew even as an infant that this mother was performing a very terrible act by keeping me in this symbolic child torture pen, in conclusion, remember I was prohibited from enjoying any kind of toys.

I was prohibited from enjoying any friendship as she made sure to remind me that I was not worthy of friendship, and especially not hers. I actually learned to be a good actor in that pen she maniacally devised, because this little boy I was made her believe that I actually was enjoying myself with these ants and bones, ha ha, a child learns to fight back. We all were raised by parents or leastwise most of us, but this little boy would have to learn to survive his, & I knew to admit that I could never enjoy myself or enjoy toys would be to admit to this sick twisted religious zea lot type mother defeat. To admit to this religiously bent & twisted mother would be equal to going back to having to eat feces with the others & then have to endure her nurturing me back to health, but what if she wouldn't be able to. Often times I ask myself, did I have a Munchausen's syndrome mother?

A SIBLING WHO WILL HAVE TO GO UNNAMED IS MY SALVATION

I know that I was in this mini-dungeon of my mom's devising for quite a long time because one sister would check on me sometimes with my mother at her side & other times she would sneak me little tidbits of food, but they were always very meager. But it was the vote of support that this represented that was my real nourishment. I didn't care that she brought me very little, but it was the act that of even being able to talk to anyone other than this terrible mother that really sustained me. Sorry sis, that I called you stingy on these occasions but it was true & you were fat to me & already I was very skinny & truly starving to death, but she had also gone thru this so this made this terrible act so so dismissible to this also tortured victim of this so called mother, but I don't want to remind these siblings about these terrible memories so again, I'm going to omit pointing any fingers, we were all children. Although we were all children, I still have to admit, these were all older siblings & I was still the very smallest of this 5 & if it had not been for this sister at great danger to herself, for had she been caught, she would have got worse than I was getting, at this time there was no father to intervene, he must have been out gambling, womanizing or out on a drunk for many months. Now I want to get back to how I started out this paragraph & it was how I know now like I always have known that I was in this pit for a very protracted time is the comment made by this cute and sometimes also troublesome sis', and it was "mom, I think we better let him out now, because just look how much he's grown," and I remember her frightened wide eyes.

Many of the defects I still have today I didn't have before I was forcibly placed in this dirt pit. I'll try to list many of them, but I know that they won't all be remembered, because I know that there are too many, so please forgive but, if I publish another volume to this terrible story, I'll mention them in it and make sure to make reference to the fact that I am trying to be all inclusive.

When I was finally discovered by what is left of humanity in this horrible dungeon I now have developed terrible tremors that I didn't have when I'm put in there.

After about a couple of months these tremors go away for the most part but to this day whenever I yawn, I have quite a bit of convulsions until I stop yawning, and I clearly remember this trembling never happened when I yawned before this imprisonment, & my siblings complained to this mother that she had now ruined their only other little brother & they further complained that they had been made to wait so long for me a boy to finally come along and now she had done this to the one tiny little brother that these siblings had grown to love so much. "I guess this is why I still love these siblings to this day and these are and were the memories that did sustain me when I was down there so just having this knowledge in my head was what prevented me from giving in to the torture mother, felt something changed my mother into some kind of monster." '^when I was still free up above this pit that was mine now all of us 5 kids were told there was only going to be enough food for 4 plus the adults so one of us 5 were going to be chosen to go to the torture pit so guess who was chosen, only my favorite sis, the one that got away with sneaking me her priceless stingy tidbits, so you know I wasn't going to be able to live with myself if she went in there so I volunteered to go there in her place & I almost knew what this entailed, but I didn't. This is when I get really indoctrinated to this full dose of her loving torture nature. Obviously, if I'm writing about this event, this is what is agreed upon with mommy dearest. That mother paled in comparison to mine. If I had the choice today, I'd still go in her place, I really don't think she would have been able to withstand this kind of treatment that she must have gone thru before herself as she was terrified at the prospect. As I already was familiar with this mother's antics, I felt I might be more able to withstand her ratings than this adorable sister.

One time at night mom didn't lock the trap door so I got out in the middle of the night and I hadn't ate in a long long time so I raided the fridge then the next day my mom had a cow because I was all satisfied so that must have been when she decided to extend my imprisonment indefinitely! I also got to get her tongue lashing, "now you've ate all the food and now all the other have nothing to eat, so she continued, "and now you aren't even going to get those juicy bones," to that I say some juicy! Well folks, at least she would still provide water. Picture that not even bread and water, literally, & I'm not trying to be Southern either, but I'd a been happier with the bread being included. I only did that one more time and I couldn't eat enough to be found out and I couldn't possibly leave any bones or crumbs as evidence! In conclusion, this dearest sister never got caught sneaking me those mere tidbits which isn't what kept me alive but the human contact did though. After I got removed from this living hell nightmare, none of us ever got placed in there again. This took the Police (in the form of a social worker as she was dressed in plain clothes though she had a file and had filled out a report) On this day I was made to lie to this so called social worker and it makes me mad even today although it shouldn't because this clerk to me now made me choose between being farmed out to foster parents and this meant all of us kids or being able to keep this mother but I had to sign either of two documents, or reports. In one it stated that she hadn't done many of a host of abuses which I had enumerated to her, and the other would include these childhood tortures that I have managed to survive. This clerk did take the time to carefully explain the consequences of signing either one. In other words the power of breaking up our precious family of 5 rested in my lap, but I truly didn't have to even think about this as I shuddered at the prospect of being farmed out to a faceless stranger that wouldn't know, me from Adam. This clerk was a white woman & to me I had already been offended by some white people already so even at this tender age of almost 3 or so, this woman represented an evil white person that didn't want to tell me everything and this just made me leery of her so I lied and signed the document which released her of all culpability so that I could keep this biological torture mother. I had a feeling that if I had let this clinical lady that was starting to get cross with me at my indecision an answer soon, soon the choice wasn't going to be mine, in other words, this bigger than life to a little tyke was about to take the choice away from me. I also did have a distinct sense that this white woman had disdain for me because this was a poverty destitute situation & my mother was waiting in the wings but she wasn't crying or anything like that but making comments to the effect, "I frankly don't care what you or he does, just get me away from this situation & me the hell away from all these child monsters that area doing nothing but eating me out of house & home, and never listen or obey their mother. This mother obviously was having some kind of nervous breakdown. Wait till you read about the lengths that this mother states to us kids that she's willing to go to, to get rid of us as you read in later chapters.

I have absolute conviction that from this cruel unconscionable treatment of me my life was changed forever. I now know that the time I spent in that hole was up to 6 months of my very vulnerable formative years that is gone forever and indelibly etched in my mind until I die. This book is helping considerably as this will tell the world how the abuses of an infant can come to haunt those that did these things or ultimately the society at large which had allowed this to happen. The crux of the problem just might have been this disdain that this white clinician had for us this Hispanic family, I later grew up only in this very same community for the remainder of my childhood and adolescence. German Township is the name of the neighborhood where this happened to me. I however won't disclose where exactly. it is but only say that it's known as the heartland the Midwest of this our United States and I was their native son, but I was just a brown one to these clinicians who serviced this area of many Germans although there other white race ethnics like Irish and French, this was mostly Germans that were enjoying the American dream yet it seems to me now that these same local Social workers did nothing to improve my life accept cause me to stay with this torture mother and MOMMY DEAREST would resume her torture of these she called unruly troop she referred to us from time to time. My tiny vulnerable soul would now go onto almost without acceptation totally be her object of abuse, torture, cruel psychological abuse where here main taunts were that I was a total weight and produced nothing or was worthless and gave nothing to the family and only ate all their food. I was effeminate & wasn't as good as my older brother, 7 yrs. older, how could a 2 or 3 yr. old compete with one that was 10? In short this mother's favorite psychological abuse wasn't at all different than the psych ridicule abusive taunts that these stupid low class self proclaimed Redneck Raiders that are hold up next door in the adjacent apt. and I'm not ashamed to say this as this 2012 and unlike her that's dead now, to me these creeps are only a representation of her hatred of this soft nature in us that we all have inside. I believe that everybody wants to be treated with to making gentleness and tenderness, but this mother was **determined**' some kind of little goos stepping tiny soldiers out of our brood. Sin embargo, (although) this mom's abuses were interminably drilled into us, because I already had memories about her were she'd for example take away my teddy bear at my age of 1, and tell me that she threw him in the garbage, to me it was absolutely survival nature in me now to now listen to this crazy one that could do this to an infant & his teddy bear, not to mention the crack to my skull that was still very fresh in my memory so, I would defy this mother or I might die, and that's the way a 1 year olds mind works, like it or lump it.

MY WHAT SEEMS TO ME STARK ABUSE ONLY GETS MORE DIABOLICAL

Actually my horrific abuse starts in the crib, that's where I received my meat cleaver crack to my head. Mom was about 4 yards away from me & she seemed to be practicing hitting a target with some kind of knife, later I'd find out alright that this deadly knife was in fact a meat cleaver & later she would reason that my head was misshapen so she was taking a chance by breaking this skull to reshape it, but as it turned out at the age of 11months, this is too late to reshape a head, and anyway, this is not the kind of way that one goes about to perform what ought to be done in a hospital if such an operation were done. Do you think for one minute that I think that this act was justified any way?

The following account is in all trueness the very way that I remember how she did this to me. At just about the time I put it together, that she was practicing to crack me in the skull and I was standing in my crib which was also my bed, this terrible mother sneaks up on me when my back was turned away from her when she had me. She had caught me off guard when I felt a super hard crack to the right side of my head just above my right ear and about 2 inches back. Blood started gushing out and I started to fall but I caught myself & told my mom that she probably wasn't going to be able to fix this injury as I already knew this mom & I knew that she was probably capable of this, I had already had needles stuck right in the same area directly into the skull and I had managed to complain to her to stop this treatment of me which I didn't understand, but I did know that this was wrong. Mom started blubbering and as she saw that this wasn't going to kill me, so she assured me that she was going to get right on it and proceeded to construct a wrapping of my head and managed to get away with having done this and my siblings didn't find out as I slept upstairs in the crib the same room with mom and dad that is whenever dad would decide to be there, what a mother, as just as it was dawning on me that this cretin was about to actually carry out this threat of reshaping my head in this manner, she did catch me her child she also knew her weaknesses, you see she was sharper than an 11 mo. old well, whoopee for her, bully for her, emphasis on BULLY. After that injury, that took several months to recover from, I ended up with slurred speech, lisping which also went away about 1 yr. or so later, but I always heal, yet additional to these defects she's creating by inflicting these injuries, I later will develop the tremors that don't go away for about 3 to 4 weeks and only show up now when I yawn, but boy I was scared there for a while as well as my siblings were, but this did go away. My defects that I've mentioned be greatly added to as time goes on. I don't know whether it was from lack of proper nutrition, or also from the crack on the head, but the mother would regularly reinforce to us children that she was like God and she could fix anything. In fact, this issue of my head had been discussed with me as if a child such as myself would know enough to reason about such medical things & I would always come back with I never want you to try to do such a thing to reshape my head, this sounded crazy to me, because even though I was a tyke, I did possess enough common sense to know better than this kind of procedure could potentially be fatal if not done by a doctor.

At the bleak and scarceness time when I'm hold up in the access crawl space only for plumbing maintenance I clearly remember I developed self injury & ticking mannerisms that I never had before this childhood incarceration and I still live with these defects from these injuries and isolation and negligence which I now know was criminal negligence of the severest kind! Today the more stress I'm under, the more I self bite within my mouth and I usually do bleed and these inner cuts take 3 to 5 days to heal. Lately, when I went thru closing down a trailer park that I bought in 1989 due to the terrible economic downfall of 2010, I ended up lisping again but this time it is due to the ticking that my precious mother inflicted on me at my tender age of 2. I've been called a great achiever by some in my life before, but even people that have done great things can come apart and be undermined by the lower elements of society, & my job is to not allow these lower elements of conspirators, racists, and all of their similar affiliates get to me, but coupled with still these childhood injuries I can & will still hurt myself, but writing this book is the best way that I'm going to get back at these creeps who are always claiming that they aren't going to relent until I'm ruined*

These ill and probably mentally injured of society self proclaimed types had better watch out for me who has gained the name, the come

15

back kid dubbed by my beloved cousins of whom only one still lives today and I also regard her with total love so I hope if this book makes decent money, I'll be granting several sums of money to these relatives that thought enough of me to include me even if only in this passing way. This cousin remembered how when 19 yrs. old and I had a severe nervous breakdown that lasted more than a year then suddenly, I snapped out of it. Thus, the come back kid. Love you Lucinda.

Now that I'm older, I know this was a minor concussion, and I was able to speak still so I said in Spanish to my mother, "you really did it now mom, I guess you win unless I live after some bandage help is given, are you going to get one?" I can still feel the warm sticky hotness of my blood and remember how terrified that this so called mother that was doing this to me looked. I pondered how I could I really be her actual son? This was the ultimate betrayal by one that is supposed to be nurturing me yet mostly what I remember at this tender age is an awful lot of arguing by me and her after she told me that my innocence is gone and I was told that I wasn't a child anymore. My head was then wrapped in gauze, (the eternal Florence Nightingale/nurse) then she assured me that I was going to be OK, in between her blubbering and she was going to nurse me back to health, a theme I witnessed her perform way more times than I care to remember. The others were the ones that succumbed much more than I did with regards to this behavior of continually needing to be nursing back these constantly ill older siblings. Now, in retrospect as I think back on this, this tends to convince me that mom suffered from a form of Munchhausen's syndrome. The area of my head that I was struck at is approximately where the area of the brain controls compulsive behavior, so I learned from watching a documentary about a serial killer similar to Jeffry Dahmer. Sometimes I ask myself was the other side of this Gemini mother, the monster that Gemini's are known to have to live with. Was she trying to injure this side of my head intentionally to create this type of defective behavior as not much control with regards to compulsive behavior. Did this diabolical mother have a plan for me to be some kind of compulsive creature of her intentional making? Later as you read on, you also may begin to see truly little clue a that seem to point to a mother that is so intelligent, I witnessed her tutoring my egghead brother on advanced algebra, I saw much to my surprise this mother typing at about the speed that I would take 7 yrs. to attain, and this mother was also almost always counting as she was either knitting, crocheting, sewing, or even designing highly intricate doilies that were so beautiful that my sister and brother found suitable for framing. To this day-these framed doilies decorate my sis's walls & I still enjoy seeing them whenever I visit them. Did all of my many injuries and extreme isolation and deprivation make me become something like these aforementioned serial types only one that vowed to never commit such a thing like to kill a living being? I knew that there was no way of getting at her and all the others that were so privileged to have plenty to eat, plenty of companionship, plenty of comfortable furniture, plenty of other of things to drink besides water & no bread even. In ancient times, I'm told even our prisoners were afforded the luxury of bread to go with their meager water, but I would not be, and Sothern's, have your good laugh, this great joke is played on one from the society you hate most, MEXICANS and you bet I'm a Chicano. Now let's see If you're going to dispossess me of my last and only antique trailer where I have my last possessions that are totally personally mine and only personal to me, family pictures, family gifts, etc. I won't put this past them as they're constantly being egged on by Redneck Raiders, due to my nervous breakdown.

Yes I did say nervous breakdown, and this unique mother who also was in fact a graduate nurse had a history of quite a few nervous breakdowns of her own. Was this a genetic defect that I would inherit from this DEMON mother or did ill behavior that I also would feel compelled to develop actually be the outcome and result of these terrible abuses that I was experiencing at her hand throughout my life. Are you my readers going to be the Judges, Jury and maybe even Executioners, you better not try to kill me after what I've been thru, I feel like I've been killed and come back more already more times than again I care to remember. I currently have lived in the South part of the U.S. for a very long time and have invested much of my life and am just like most all Americans suffering the same economic woes as any body else and currently, the mood by us here in FL is every dog for themselves more than ever before. I really believe had we not had such terrible downturns, I never would have been inclined to have to write this terrible book in just such a way. America, I am not writing this book to titillate, stimulate, or be sensationalistic, but am forced to turn to writing this terrible acct. of a life of abuse to see if in doing so, my finances would then be in the turn around and recovery mode. I know that that sounds like I view things like potentially anything or everything probably has a dollar sign on it with me, but trust me I already have enough assets and this is affording me the time to go forward with the writing this I hope to be the greatest work of art of my life. Do bear in mind that I was forced to be the torture child or whatever I was in this achievement oriented family so I have learned to adapt and have had considerable College education.

In so stating that I too achieved a high level of High Ed, I as a reader would be getting goose bumps at the thought of this, but how do you suppose anyone was going to learn to adapt in such an achievement oriented family? I'll get back to this in later chapters, but I digress to when I just posed the question, "Did this mother deliberately injure me as she bragged she had considerable anatomical studying which is included with her nurse diploma, was she seeking to damage the area that controls compulsiveness, etc. remember that question I posed, well, Maybe my lot in life was to enjoy a little bit of genetic inherited (her mental illness, & nervous breakdowns, then she had to add the physical injuries to this particular area of the brain so does the reader begin to see any patterns and or similarity to this mother yet? Maybe I had a little bit of both, are you getting titillated, ha? This is how horrible I regard this so called upbringing. Now I have to get back to after my blow to my head.

Now after I healed from that strike on the head I changed in a couple ways, I hope I remember them all. One of the most dramatic ways that I changed was I now had become quite untrusting & she would name this neurotico (neurotic) what do you expect! I now become somewhat impulsive and compulsive as I learn and grow up. Due to this type of behavior with many nervous mannerisms, OCD is now evident, she obviously wants to hide this injured child that is me. This is when my lonely part of my life begins so this stranger type mother now informs me from now on she is going to always try to isolate me from the rest of the precious perfect prodigy children (she'd say) as if I had performed this injury upon myself. She then carried out this promise alright and I rarely had any playmates & then basically I grew up alone, lonely, and yes ISOLATED. Here I must interject that the older kids were allowed to snipe put downs at me though, and when these co-abused older children would talk to me, they'd use her put downs & tactics. This assured they'd get more food, freedom, & rewards with her bragging how her children (just not me she'd pipe in) were truly gifted over achievers/prodigies, but she left out; bullies, selfish, conceited & the list goes on but they almost all did turn out to be dynamic super achievers, and even including myself in the final analysis, after all I am capable of writing this complete story all by myself without a single assistance from any of these so called super children of hers that hardly ever call me unless they might need this or that signed.

Remember, I had these children that she sometimes recounted such grown up with tales to us like, "I knew of a woman that was able to design her children to each one be a specific part and play a very special role and was able to rule an entire country in this manner. Now couldn't I be this kind of mother and I truly read about this so wouldn't you like to be this kind of world controlling super-children that I would have made?" Maybe this mother did have her grand master plan, who am I to say, it just seems to me from all of my memories, that she forgot to include enough love for all. I'll go a step further and state that she went to the extreme and went on to not provide any love at all for some of us, we were always craving reassurance from her and asking her if she loved us, and we all did this, not just this one or that one.

ALL PSYCHOSIS DISSIPATES WHEN THIS EDIFICE TYPE MOTHER PASSES I'm still a little compulsive today but nothing like I was eleven 11 yrs. ago when this living torture mother was still living so the truth be known, the comparison could be something like I'm 85% abnormally compulsive before she dies, then within 4 months after she dies, I'm suddenly down to less than 2% abnormally compulsive, this felt like I had been released from her shackles upon my soul. I was so trying to come back to some kind of sensibleness to my life when she dies on me)leaving me with no closure as to why had she had hurt me in so many different ways, this I'll have to take to my grave I guess, never knowing why this mother treated me so terribly when I could have been treated in all of the right ways that she started to be when I 1st. was coming to the realization that this was the parent that I was to regard as my mother. at this beginning when a child is 1st. self realizing coming alive to the world and well, just firstly opening up his eye§ at this very beginning, my mom was OK, but it would be within this 1st. yr. of life that I would begin to see the twisted torture nature of this mother who lovingly I will refer from time to time as Florence Nightingale. In conclusion even as I age and try to stay connected with this the only family I've known, I still attribute this ill behavior to her constantly egging me on as if to suggest that because I'm still not being one of her super children who were Christian, & of course it wouldn't matter whether I made it up there for the Yuletide or

not, after all, I had made my bed she'd say, so I ought to lay in it. She liked
to add, you don't practice this region anyway so come if you can make it,
but it shouldn't matter to you now should it?" Can you believe that I'm
still trying to win back this mother's love and now, I'm 47 Yrs. old already,
but this cold and human less mother was somehow unreachable as far as
being emotionally available. Maybe this is why it was my sister who came
instead of my mom to help take care of me once when I went under the
knife & now come to think of it, I after I had had operations in the past
now knew better than have this mother anywhere in the area, what was I
thinking? The worst thing that this mother did for me was love me in the
1st. very 1st. few months of life before starting with the probing into the
skull with some kind of huge very pointed needles. Sin embargo, I'm just
opening my eyes, I know when I'm being injured by this soon to show
me that she was sick up in the upper story to do this to me and I'm just
starting to realize the horror of what life is just about to become. The way
she'd throw things, the way that cruel sis Baby Jane threw things at her
helpless sister, is how she would act when she was coming undone and I
knew then even as a tyke that she was apt to hurt me so I was careful not
to let my guard down. Later when I grew to about 3^ my mom regarded
me too strong already if I'd need to put up a fight so one of the ways she
found would work to subdue me sin embargo, I may have been in a deep
sleep, but I was to wake up bound and in a situation that I was unable to
get out of, so many times she would use the old tie them up while they're
asleep routine to trap me for example the time I was put in the plumbing
space below the bathroom for one, nevertheless (sin embargo) I had to
have discipline and or her torture so my deep sleep was the least of this
sad bitches worries.

Going back to right after the death of this mom, this is when it seems
all of the threats she had made to me in my life seemed to just suddenly
melt away as if someone had waved a major wand. Had my mind or what
was left of at this time rationalized that now the threat of a discipline
mother to the nth degree has now been removed. sin embargo, a self made
abandoned son still will survive whether you give him closure or not. This
sinister threat of a selfish and self centered self serving and abusive to the
point of absurdity is over,-. Not even the talks on the phone telling me
that I don't measure up to her Christian other siblings when at the funeral
I heard them complain that I had outdone them all, and was I always
competing with them to be the best one to prove to her that I more than

measured up, probably, as I knew at the back of my mind that nothing less would be good enough for her.

WILL I AS MY LIFE ACCOMPLISHMENT BE CAPTAIN AMERICA 'S SCAPEGOAT

If when I'm thru writing this true story, surrealistic as it may appear a horrific acct. of a life as I find out that it apparently must be OK for a mother to treat her child this way in this country. Albeit I think I always knew that it wasn't just the same I was treated these ways that I've been describing so far. Now if America did this to her native son, "This kind of treatment throughout my entire life while she lived wasn't OK with me as witnessed by my subsequent paying back by way of acting out terribly as I became demented and felt such things as torture this America that did this to you back.

MOTHER CAT CAN KILL ANY OF A LITTER SHE PERCIEVES A THREAT

One of mom's famous threats, "I have to become the same way that a cat is to keep the strongest of the litter alive, even if it means having to kill one or a couple of them." After time passes on and I have several injuries that I survive, this cat mother started to perceive me as her weak kitten. So mother would say something like "remember the runt of the litter that mother cat knows she has to do away with to save the rest of the stronger ones?" This creepy mother would recount, "The mother cat in her infinite wisdom all knowing about being a mother, knows she has to snuff the runt out so that the others that are stronger have a much better chance at living and thriving. WOW, what an award winning mom. Let's give her the best mom award. To tell this anecdote was one her favorite psychological torture but I guess this makes this Florence Nightingale mum a 1940's 50's version of a possible child torturer of mid-evil type torture/abuse as she especially liked to interject that she had personally witnessed a mother cat do this in person so we needed to regard her as this type of mother. Why was this mother talking in this way to tiny toddler tyke infants!

Consequently, I ended up divorcing myself from this sorry excuse of a mother. Once after lengthy conversations it was decided to offer me a different home to grow up at, that of a number of different relatives. The one that I favored over all was my sweet great aunt Genoveva of Some town in the Midwest. This was a 230 mile drive or more and all of us went as a family trip too. This cute old aunt I already knew and loved as she had found out that her sister lived in the same state as she did so these two oldsters reconnected and she had came and stayed for a couple of visits, and the two bonded again like seeing two long lost little girls reunite. I so loved the grandma that raised me really whenever this mom wasn't this grandma always was, so of all people, I chose her to be the one to finish raising as now & forever after I chose this grandma, I would never regard this mother as the real mother that would love me unconditionally the way granny did.

Getting back to the mother who liked to depict so terrible scenarios as if to instill terror one time I clearly remember her talking to this illiterate father that I am supposed to believe is my real true father, "If you continue to behave badly like the womanizing drunk and neglect these your kids, I could use them as my human guinea pigs as you do remember that I am a nurse and know a lot about experimentation and these children are perfectly intact so I could see how I could cause certain changes in them thru experimentation," this I know by the look of horror in his eyes, as dad was an illiterate and he would always come across this childlike innocent way to me, even when I would grow up. So, he counter with something like, "You'd never do something like that to our beautiful little group of babies, would you, & of course this mother gave him her ICE MAIDEN COLD look I would later coin and dub her, this torture mother. Maybe this father was yet unaware of the tortures this torture mother herself must have endured, so this mother found that much easier to be able to administer her famous tortures which she bragged about how she was knowledgeable about in enough ways from her being a member of her girlfriends torture club, so she would tell me.

Yet, after witnessing such kind of dialogue between a so called father and mother that were supposed to be completely responsible for my well being, and when I'd see the look in this father's eyes, it seemed like a sinister portent to a tiny little 2^ yr. old that I was, what do you expect me to feel/ maybe y'all feel like the Sothern's where I ended in the later part of my productive life, that I got what I deserved because I was this soft and gentle little boy child, why this type needs to be tough ended up and let's throw in a little torture for good measure besides a good smattering of deprivation and super starvation. Such views of course aren't shared by most I surmise in the South, but as I lived here in an impoverished neighborhood, as you may know, the lower down the socio-economic ladder, the less tolerance that is shown towards what these poor substance abusing and devoid of higher education types with racism as motto will view as. This type is ruled by cult type mentality, as I view these types this way. It doesn't matter to me that some of them may have a smidgen of education, or even considerable education, they would still be following a cult type mentality for the purpose of brainwashing the same way that Adolf Hitler was able to create a cult type mentality that he almost ruled the world with. We all were going to be having to give a Sieg Heil, I can't believe I defiled this book by even writing it down on these pages leastwise those that were white enough to be allowed to live.

WAS THIS MOTHER WHO ALSO BRAGGED GRADUATED AT THE TOP CONSCIOUSLY FULL KNOWING SHE WANTED TO CREATE HER OWN DOMMER

If so, folks, she was far ahead of her time, I just didn't particularly want to be that Dahmer and you know now from reading herein already that she knew a hell of a lot about anatomy as she was a graduate nurse, imagine that!

NEWSFLASH

"Now I'm hearing these creepy neighbors (the set up by sleazy trailer park I own raid probably) someone's crying, "I'm afraid to apply for the deed to my trailer that's parked in this particular red neck concern's trailer park, & they own several of them in this town, but anyway, "to move forward on trying to claim his antique project trailer a Zimmer due to I have no money & they know until I receive my dad's inheritance in July. Why would somebody right next door to where I live here be saying such things about me and my life? This to me seems to speak of conspiracy!

Anyway, I'm the one that thru writing this book, will bring this cycle of abuse throughout my life up to and including the writing of these lines as I consider these raiding around me a mere part of this ongoing invasion of my life. Basically, that is certainly what's going on as I've heard people discussing how to sabotage my life ever since I can remember, so even now as I write these lines, I know that the person or persons watching me do this are an ongoing part of this the invasion of my life that this book stops the cycle, that's so a part of that tortured childhood, period.

Now, these functional illiterate types, that I hear reading these lines, as I write and type, I make stop as I have reported them to everybody from the FBI TIP LINE ON CRIMINAL ACTIVITIES/ORGANIZED CRIME, THE (OUR WHITE HOUSE-OBAMA'S), THE NATIONAL COUNCIL OF LA RAZA, yes, I'm Mexican American, but this is a true story of what happened and is happening in my life.

The list goes on, as I've contacted quite a few other organizations. I have already gone as far as making an announcement of this, my forthcoming book. Another reason that I don't have any qualms about telling about this kind of shocking story about extreme child abuse and severe sub-human deprivation is largely due to the fact that most anything these days isn't even shocking anymore. It's as if we've become these stoic human less unfeeling creatures that are well, it just seems that we as humankind as a whole, are disconnected from our actual selves as if we no longer possessed any kind of feelings, we would rather be thrilled, titillated, stimulated by the bazaar rather than wholesome things. How have we gotten this way & would we like to be the recipients of the kind of abuse and injuries in this book? I never did want to be a scapegoat, bulls eye, and buried alive child as a part of a twisted game of a mom and her 5 children. Wait till you read later about how I describe the events lead-up to the distinction of being about 3 yrs. old when I was buried alive. But don't forget, I'm the youngest of the brood.

NOW MOMMY DEAR HAS TO TRAIN HER SUPERCHILDREN TO BE PERFECT Mom would root them on & with me in mind, "she wasn't fooling me", she'd say something like, "Would you all say as loudly as you can for me just how full you are & just maybe Julian will hear you and decide to listen and learn to obey everything I say." They would all try to outdo one another to be the loudest one for this mean, cruel, vicious CAT who kills the runt mother, but this mother is going a step further & creating a runt, was this possibly due to all these times already and up to this tender age of 3 yrs. injuries that I've already sustained? I only know and vividly remember that this mother who could and had sneaked up and hit this earlier child that I was when I was in the crib, and after this had given to an older uncle in exchange for paying the rent, as the only father that I knew would be gone and this older man who lived in the upstairs of our house was also an illegal alien and was hiding from our law enforcement. Yet I would still like to know why I was provided to this uncle at about 11 mo's along with room & board, I would be included, this was OK with me as I already had the sense that I didn't get along with this mother too well. Still fresh are the memories of the sharp 4in. needles right thru the skull right into the brain! Why should I listen to a brutal mother who can switch from a loving and caring one to that of one that is so filled with hate I guess I cermised by this time. I had seen her mislead my younger siblings on so many occasions that at times it would make me laugh, I saw humor in this mother's behavior, then at other times she seemed to change so dramatically she didn't seem like the mother that I knew, but was a total stranger to me. NOW as I think back, this paints a picture of a mother that suffers from some kind of schizophrenia, and also, in retrospect there are many memories that pointed to drug abuse, (heroine) and later she even informed us that she at one time in her life had no choice but to self-administer morphine due to liver disease she had developed. Anyway, this terrible mother also derived pleasure from seeing her very own children suffer or have to hear the privileged b ones brag about how full they are & this gave her a laugh, but at my expense, as I'm from what I remember the one that was always deprived of much to eat, so I grew this elongated stomach, and not from eating a lot, but from Biafra type stark starvation. Yet, I would still have to bear hearing after I was placed against my 2 yr. old infant's will in a shallow pit without any light at all the happy sounds of my older siblings above hearing my bro's and sisters running around above freely, joyously, playfully, laughing & sometimes yes, boasting about how much they had eaten, how overstuffed full they were, and asking when I was going to be let out, to have the Bitch say "If I do, my plan will be ruined & you all won't get enough to eat as he eats the most like a pig, that's when you all starve, don't you remember?" My little brothers and sisters were probably right to agree with her but then they didn't know anything about child abuse & torture & negligent rape, childhood human traffic, was I this mother's child sex doll to an illegal homosexual uncle? "Sin embargo, this criminally mischievous mother that probably was doing drugs from now having become addicted, had these siblings of mine thinking that to let me free and out again meant they would not eat enough, "Such are the life and times of stark poverty culture children & a mother o of the early mid 50's whose husband is nowhere to be found, probably this is what the main dysfunction was, a womanizing mate, that was an Itinerate job hunter until he found steady work for the railroad, and went from seasonal to permanent year round employment. Now this when our situation stops being so dismal, I even remember one or two Christmases that the older ones had gifts. HOW DID SUCH A MOTHER GET TO ENJOY TORMENTING INFANTS?

My 1st memories of abuse were either spending an entire day, and this would happen often, the entire day without having my diaper changed & then walking bowlegged, this kept the do do off better, or the time I was left in a hot car in summer way too long, or when this mother would stick needles into my head as I'm sure I've already described. This mother now looked at me like I was an enemy & I really didn't know why or for what reason. The one time that she did this it went like this? Mother looked very clinical as she was caught off guard as thru my peripheral vision I saw her curious expression and I almost could read her mind & a child can know by many of her previous quirky behavior that things are summing up to be an apparent behaving parent, the mother trying to save more food, warmth and etc. the way the cat mom does when she has to snuff out the one to better save the stronger of the litter. This theme this parent would repeat thru out the childhood I would experience until 19 yrs. of age even after I had left the nest, this mother insists of psychological abuse with possibly physical abuse thru surgery on me this son she tortured this way all her life and she has gotten away with it! I could see in her expression that she was weighing our or measuring how much she thought I was able to withstand but I with' stood no more than once at least by the time I caught on, cause I actually didn't feel them but just go straight in then straight out, but then she pulled away and practiced in the air as if rehearsing what she was about to do, then I took her hand, stopped her and demanded that she remove this, one that had gotten by me but she would say, "I can do anything I want with you, you're my possession, my property & I'd say, "No, you can't, you cant do THAT, so I decided then I'd see if she might have feelings on her head, "ha" like she'd laugh, and when my bottle was empty & or it had sour milk which made me mad too, but I waited until I was hungry and mad also still stewing about needles into my skull, I took my sour bottle and thru it straight bulls eye at her head & hit her square to teach her that must hurt on the head and after that, this is when I got the meat cleaver to the head, and brain, I was about 11 to 13 months old

NOW THE REAL GOOD STUFF OF ABUSE, TORTURE, ISOLATION JUST STARTED

I know this is such a sad sad story to tell, but It's one that has to be written as such things as us Americans are coming to terms with things like the trial of the Anthony mother. Just think, during, this horrible story that I witnessed on television I set about writing this, my story and you wouldn't believe the parallel's that I saw between what the little girl went thru and the guilty look on her mother reminded of when mom had to talk to the social worker that filled out that file, in which I was made to lie or I don't know who or what I would have for a parent 1

At times when writing this true account, my hands tremble & sweat profusely, I've actually built up the courage to face up to this horrible and injurious almost all encumbering mess of a childhood. I know this is going to sound completely the blame game, but I will show how self abuse that is a learned self defense mechanism can also evolve into the psychological aspect of the human makeup may also go haywire this way. Specifically, a behavior that could be construed as serial behavior may and can stem from such mistreatment of the psychological development of something so precious as a tiny infants mind.

Do you think that something like compulsive flashing or indecent exposure could stem from having been locked up in a torture cell by such cruelty and evil viciousness by a doped up mother as punishment but which went on for months could lead to such apparent behavior. Sin embargo, this little boy that really didn't think the way the mother does, "Nevertheless, I deserved crueler punishment than was allowable by law, by far, bound and gagged, drugged up, starved in the most critical developmental stage, "Now, people, it came to my mind like some brainstorm, that there would be a way that I might be able to call attention of all of the aforementioned abuses that were going on at the time. The thing that came to me that I could do so someone would come and save me from these abuses that were leaving me mal nourished, "I had to be about 40 to 75% lacking in nutrition, and I had little to no body mass, the thing that I had to make myself have the courage to do was to run up and down the road when mom was asleep, and, now I look like I much bigger than I am, but, I was on ly about 3 to 4, old enough to know better, but then, after that, another social worker would come to question me, and then after this, my mother assured the officer that none of the above that I had said in the form I didn't sign would happen either and that's how the state would leave it so she could keep her children.

This running up and down the road at the front of our house, in broad daylight bare naked, saved my life as after that I was treated only marginally better, shortly after which this compulsive torture with her

27

propensity to be ever more torturous and creative would return to her old ways.

In a sense, I am hoping that the writing of this book fixes my life as I only want to make it right with my American family, and I hope and pray that those who read my account of my life will be able to see how a helpless injured child has to learn to survive. Any terrible acting out of mine that offended anybody was nothing more than a manifestation of mine to self destruct at what I misguidedly thought was the worlds fault, when those who were at fault were the torturer's, abuser's and criminally neglectful of me America, your native son. As I move to the South later in life, I'm treated terribly by the FL Govt. and it seems to me my mistreatment is ongoing, so this becomes my switch that this backward local town pulls, they press the wrong buttons, by an entrapment arrest, then later an arrest without mirandized so I'm being treated like some subhuman thing without any rights as if I wasn't even an American! Add to this getting stuck when I and my life mate buy a trailer park that is purported by some slum junk yard dweller that I'm not welcome in his neighborhood, speaking of hood, that's actually all that this creep is and ever will be to me. I asked him, the creep, "and what of your famed new South, isn't there a renewed mood in the South, but I was only asking this idiot in vain as he claimed he was the head of several hate groups, and why they would choose a bully that brags obnoxiously about the area being their Holy hate site dedicated to the hate groups aforementioned, is beyond me. Maybe it was because with this moron as a leader, they will lose with me, as I already have to my credit a former title of Regional Secretary for La Raza Unida an organization for the advancement & education, with courses such as English as a Second language, Job seeking training, other projects such as a Weatherization to better insulate the much under insulated old farm houses in the North, we provided jobs also in this way and we also had outreach, and many other activities that we did at La Raza. Today, this grass roots created by us Mexican Americans, has grown into a political power unrivaled by any other Mexican American organization, further, It is now a powerful Political Organization and us Chicanos can count on having a voice and a powerful force in this U.S. country of ours. We not only are your or our own friendly and powerful neighbor by way of Mexico, but we are also here in the good old U.S. OF A and we are your fully naturalized citizens as we Chicano's were born here, that's why we're

Chicano's, that word means we Just like anybody are capable of being the ugly American too! The dominant and main thing we are is American!

BANDS OF RACISTS OF EVERY DESCRIPTION FOLLOW ME AROUND INCESSANTLY DUE TO MY WRITING THIS BOOK

Notwithstanding these white terrorists that claim that they are these threatening hate mongering groups, and I am their poster child for Gay persecution, please bear in mind that this book isn't about them but about the plight between my sorry upbringing, but, it's just that have tried so hard to get in my way, that, I have no choice but to give them mention as they truly believe that the treatment that I got from my sorry community and parents should have been what I should have got. I absolutely know that the ill abuses that I have endured won't be the thrilling victory cry for hate groups, I cannot allow them to feel this terrible way, but then just what are they, "they are our own American neighbors that spew nothing but hate and promote and per pirated lies, propaganda, and discourage higher education to their ignorant followers, instead their legions should follow these self proclaimed saviors of humanity for their white race, now you can see how ignorant their principals are, to discourage higher education ought to be a crime in this country. After all, aren't we supposed to have some of the highest Educational standards in the world? In conclusion, remember, this writer is being followed by those hate groups that we're familiar in the hopes that they are going to get to me and I won't be able to finish this book, then they think that I should go back in my shell when I had become like catatonic once for longer than a year, but folks, this is not going to be happening, I won't be escaping to the craziness safety again, as I now once and for all have conquered these monsters of the mind of my abused past, so that is out and now all of these crazy racist people sound crazier than I have ever heard them sound before. They can go to the crazy escape route if they want, but that is all over for me at the tender age of 58, there's no point to apologize for their being mentioned in my novel, but they are doing these terrible things terrorists do and can't you see as readers that as this book gains popularity, or infamy, whatever you want to call this they'll have no choice but to stop disturbing this American son and stop being the nuisances they are to me, and that's all these underlings are here!

Get this in your heads America, these thugs/racists that I have come to know in the South, have it in for most any minorities that have good financial gains and lives, and as I bought property in FL, these low class low educated told me the way it was going to be for me if I didn't let go of my RP assets that I and another gay had purchased, as they were affiliated with all the hate groups you could think of and they were going to use these hate associated Org's and I'd never be able to be successful since they were the current system in place, and to that I say HA, you're not going to affect my failure, and that's my warning! OK, enough time wasted talking about this Achilles heal that isn't going to do me in and it doesn't either.

THE UNFATHONABLE CHILD TORTURE HAPPENS HERE IN YOUR FRONT YARD

You know, now the only thing I can do is pray that after this (almost tale like account is published) my peace of mind would be for the rest of my life and permanent as by writing this might actually get back at these now dead child abusers, so I know that there's literally nothing these deceased neglectors can do! These terrible creeps who hate and revile us homosexuals to the point of making us their edict of the social group to ruin next and deny privilege and opportunity since they now have been basically banned from hastening the Blacks. The thing they forgot is that we're a much larger group & in my case I'm affiliated with much more Organizations than they are that are powerful, and not thru violent practices. I don't consider hate groups powerless, I know better than that, but I will consider them reportable so they'll also get loving mention in this my book to remove the last obstacles in my life. The truth is I know that this book of <u>MINE</u> once & for all will put these gay and Chicano haters in their place and I don't care whether I am exonerated or not, I just want that those sort (hatemonger's) will now know better than to screw with either us gay or Chicano people.

THE STUFF OF GREAT MASTERPIECES IS WHAT THIS BOOK IS ABOUT

Sensationalism, horrific accounts of abuse, survival story written by a grown up who cracked up due to a non stop (and I mean totally CRACKERS) litany of put downs, slaps and kicks to carefully aimed inner organs, (the nurse who knew anatomy), countless punches to my right arm administered by a much older brother urged on by that mother, isolation, vilification of an infant & that's just for starters goose bumpy readers, but the list goes on to such things as being prostituted as human trafficking by ones own mother, is this getting interesting yet, are you titillated and excited yet? Well, I know that as a society it's about what we're amounting to these days, so what, this that happened to me is about as interesting as watching the shadows move in my crawl space where I had nothing else to do so this was one of very few ways that I would pass the time.

You see, it's anybody's guess as to how I survived this horrific childhood with so many bruises, contusions, hematomas, and fractures, but somehow, I had the will to live so now I'm writing this true story and as I write this remember, there's the one's who would like me to crack up again, but you know it's up to me not to give this to these subversives, early-ier, I actually heard, I'm here to work on Julian, or such a thing, and I suppose that is being spoken by one of these racists in the hope that their taunts, chants, litany of put downs will work to break my fragile psyche down, I don't think that I'm that delicate, ha ha. On that, I consider the source.

IT"S MY HOPE THAT OUR AMERICAN PUBLIC ISN"T AS JADED AS I IMPLY

I'm just one gay torture story of countless many, but to those twisted demented people who derive glee & would say, "They consider these sad acts of a sorry mother actually is their divine intervention, their infant tortures, their American son that was soft and gentle merited this torture/abuse/bloody injuries," Their belief is that I should have gotten this kind of treatment, & this is one son whose life should have been ruined. I dedicate this mother as the mascot for all these illustrious hate groups, she's their heroine leastwise, this is what they're piping into this apartment as I write these lines. This horribly terrible mother I had is no doubt what drove me crazy, but her favorite cop out was "They always blame the mother, it's always the mother's fault," "Why do head doctors as she'd refer to them, always place the blame solely on the mother." This her strongest defense was totally weak to me, yet what was the point of arguing with this mother where we certainly would go round and round, only with a mother that would even say to us that she was a bad mother to us too because we were bad children that made her this way. Now you are about to get an eye opening with regards to how this mother was so self confident about her convictions on life and death even with regards to unborn children!

Loretta Florez's abortion was deliberately brought on intentionally by my mother & she made me promise that I would never talk or even allude to what this sick mother made me get involved with doing, yet it speaks of how she regards even unborn human life. For one she felt that the child shouldn't be brought into this world because this poor dependent on working as an egg gatherer had no husband to be a father to this child when it would would be born. I now was familiar with the politics of this cruel and self centered self serving mother, these employers were only my best friends parents when I'm already 14 yrs. old. This was a terrible ordeal that I had to participate in by taking her mom's witches brew so that this would induce her to have this famous miscarriage that mom would I know feel bad about for the rest of her life. I would argue that this nice family would come to adapt to the fatherless child, but this mother was hell bent on this blue eyed Mexican girl not have her reputation ruined. Mom said that this behavior of the aforementioned girl would reflect badly on our family as we were the ones that secured her this job and home that she didn't even have to pay rent to live in. she also argued that she had already a little boy out there that didn't have a father & she only got to have from time to time, so what, that's no reason to kill an unborn baby! So this gorgeous little blond blue eyed girl got pregnant out of wedlock in the mid 60's what do you expect, but I still think this forceful mother's opinion ruined the mood for the rest of the time that I knew this Loretta a friend of mine and this families. After that event, that girl stayed depressed for a very long time and never behaved the same again, but she would say that men were the ruination of her life and I think the real ruination was this selfish mother of mine imposing her views on this innocent lonely girl, it's too bad that she knew my mom who fancied herself as a modern Mex. midwife.

Loretta was tricked to take this concoction mom called her remedy, "how callous", so I ask my readers now, "Now do you believe that this heartless mother could kill her own children as she would simply think of herself as the MOTHER CAT? Just pay attention as you read and you'll see just how far this mother can take this childlike (mom's the mother cat), on a friends unborn child. Imagine at the tender age of 14 or 15, having to be pulled into a sordid mess, and was I being a part of this to try even as sick as this act was to gain this unimaginable mother's approval, the whole time, I was arguing against going to such extreme, but this mother was already accustomed to behaving/thinking in such a way. Now as I'm writing this down I have such a sick feeling in my stomach, and I truly loved and was fond of this girls other little boy! I'm sorry Loretta, I hope you didn't have the kind of trouble thinking on this as you aged as I think of this and it is one of the most terrible things that my mother caused me to be a part ofi there have been very few that I have ever shared this information with. This feeling this way is a bit absurd now as the whole population who reads this story will know about this.

I KNOW THAT BEING A PART OF THIS DISTURBING ACT TOOK ITS TOLL

It occurs to me that this kind of tragic and horrific account unfortunately is what some of our society that is sordid, morbid, or something along deranged actually likes to hear. However, I won't settle for this type of life of medieval mediocrity, as I always strove to have a better lot in life, & I still keep on trying, that's just also myself made man makeup that didn't learn from all of those stark abuses and injuries.

THIS THAT IS SUPPOSED TO BE THE COUNTRY THAT STANDS FOR FREEDOM NEEDS TO REALIZE THAT ITS RACISM STANDS FOR UNHUMANITY

If anybody somehow is thinking that I'm enjoying writing thiS horrid account of a tiny tyke all his life terrorized and abused to the point of becoming mute for 1 yr. because I would only whisper in between tears and sobs but I couldn't talk even though I was now 19 yrs. old, you may say that's ridiculous, but this did truly happen to me, and I was also agoraphobic and refused to leave the house for over a year, unimaginable to me now as I reflect back on this dark period in my life. I had the delusion that I might be discovered that I was becoming a woman but it was the fact that this was so bullied into my head that I actually believed it. This only caused me to become the clam as I had learned by now that to withdraw and become a clam could save me as this had so many times in the past. So I did not leave the house for that year, I certainly wasn't missed, and if someone would come to visit me, I would make up the excuse that I wasn't in the mood to be disturbed, boy, I underused the meaning of that word disturbed. Anyway, I became mute & refused to talk for some 14 to 18 months, and never stopped crying for the entire period, because I felt that some part of me was dying. I lost 20 Lbs. & would regularly think of ways that I could kill myself as I knew that the cat mother wanted this anyway. I'm surprised that she didn't have me committed at this time. These times when I have great lapses of time when I seem to be in a void, or black hole like when I was in the pit below all the rest of my siblings, are the times that I will refer to that are huge parts of my life that have been stolen from me and I would like this time back that I feel was robbed from me by a ruthless animal that somehow we called a mother. The father wasn't there to intervene, but technically he would be as much to blame as this corrupt mother who thought nothing of ending a life before it is even born was. To a child and even an adolescent when I made the fool mistake to return to this torture mother after I had gotten away and had now even attended 2 quarters of College at my university that I had been accepted to, time is much longer or seems to go on ad-infinitum, when you're all alone and suffering from emotional disturbances such as I was experiencing. The time in the pit when I was a tyke seemed just as long as this year and time that I refused to talk or leave the house for fear that I would be called a sissy, girlish boy, or whatever, but these were my worst-fears, how ridiculous this seems to me now, but you just can't imagine the terrible feelings that I was experiencing at those times. Please give me back the time I lost and replace them with fun and joy, from my mouth to God's ear, I'll never get those precious moments when I was a vulnerable antsy little tyke and I was made to be so offended by such a Ed Geen type mother. AMERICA, I WANT YOU TO GIVE BACK YOUR NATIVE SON WHAT YOU ALLOWED THIS CREATURE CALLING HERSELF A MOTHER TO ME TOOK AWAY FROM ME! The saddest is that these could have been a whole lot of good times, and I'm not trying to be a Tiny Tim, just little old me. At this time I was so terribly withdrawn, I missed getting to meet my only living great grandmother, but I heard my mom say that I probably wouldn't come down from upstairs to meet her as I was sick & all I'd do was cry non-stop and did she know something that could be done to help me? This mom seemed to feel that I had to be under some kind of spell, when she was probably slipping me some of her estrogen pills, remember, this mother knew a plenty about medicine and even hormone replacement, and she is now trying to stave off menopause, so this could have been what she was doing. This mother actually would cling to the idea that was better to become a woman than to be a homosexual which was the direction that I was going and she knew this but I believe that this was a response to this. Imagine that, I've had to hear all my life that this mother who thinks she has the power of Almighty God to change the gender of her own son, might actually be attempting still to do this like when I was a child and she told me that she could maybe change me into a girl since I was so unhappy with this business of being a boy! Now at the age of a tender 19 ha ha, and I'm having a nervous breakdown obviously, what else would you call this, she's making such sounds such as maybe it's not too late to make you turn into a girl if you feel like you're more as a girl than a boy, wow, people is this mother some Florence Nightingale, or what? Boy, I knew after I heard this for the last that this mother cared nothing to very little about what I had between my legs, so I decided to muster up the courage to leave the house and go to a town 40 miles a-way, to visit a dear sister that had left this terrible nest to strike out for herself and this worried my mom, so I sneaked out and made it to my cute older sister's apartment. Boy was I going to get the surprise of my life.

RUN DON"T WALK TO ESCAPE THIS REDICULOUS NIGHTMARE OF EXTENDED CHILDHOOD TORTURE THAT THIS SELF CENTERED MOTHER WANTED TO CONTINUE WITH SUCH COMMENTS OF GERNER REASSIGNMENT

At some point in this mother's plan for my so called genderal reassignment, I know full well that I would be having to say by by to my who who, if you the part of my body I'm talking about, & this mother simply suggested to me that this wasn't something that she wanted particularly to entertain details about, but I could be assured that when we would get to that point, this issue wouldn't be a problem. The hell it wouldn't be, I would reply, just how retarded and emotionally ill did this crazy mother think I was anyway, well, I can assure the readers, of this much I was sure, nobody was going to mess with my privates ever again. Prepare to be shocked on this point, as even though I got myself to snap out of this almost catatonic state, the consummate torture mother would find a way to wound this sexual organ of mine thru her pure stealth for which I would learn to resent any involvement by this mother in my life until she dies, & I firmly believe that this was just another of that mother's injuries to repel me just like the cat that wounds one of her kittens that might be a problem to her or the rest of her litter. My entire life I had to hear that a homosexual would never, and never is tolerated in Mexican society, and make no mistake people, I cannot divorce myself from being of Mex. blood, but I also am not willing to excuse this craziest reasoning to date that it is alright to reassign my gender just because I might be so inclined. Another cop out of hers was that for the time that we lived in, this kind of abuse treatment of homosexually inclined children is acceptable, but people, the time is the 50's and 60's not the middle ages and so to that I say, bull shit! "Oh by the way, the time and year that she was further messing with my genitals in later adulthood, was in the mid 70's, so, double bull"". This asking this great grandmother of mine whom I never got a chance to meet if she might know how to break such a spell, is so incongruent to all of the rest of her formal training as a nurse, just who did she think she was kidding, I already knew of her earshot ploy. Now suddenly she is of the superstitious variety, & with all of her intellectual wisdom and knowledge, this paints a picture of a very fickle and unreliant mother & only made me feel more trapped by this mother's domineering nature, who also was exhibiting still a wanting to get back at a child for I really don't care the reason, I was tired of all of my terrible memories of abuse that were the dominating force for some reason, I couldn't even get these things out of my mind. Now she's using the earshot ploy, and with the superstitious ploy too and add her coy ignorant mum that doesn't know how to deal with a situation, "I call this very scary behavior. "Oh dear, what could this mid-wife to Hispanics as she fancied herself do?" "Only fix more blame, heap more scorn/condemnation on homosexuals while all around me a gay movement has been launched, and the American Psychological Assn. has already released new determinations on homosexual lifestyle/is no longer regarded as sickness, but an al ternate lifestyle yet a deviation from the norm. One thing she could fix was blame, she's gotten good at that.

But this witch doctor mother couldn't fix the problem, she preferred fixing blame, & she certainly wasn't going to fix this blame on herself.

In actuality I thought I was thought of as an all around good guy by most all, and a simple guy, but not a girl, & I never lost sight of wanting to meet a nice country girl & maybe have a son or a daughter or even one of both. This I actually went on to do but in the frame of mind of a brave new world, I felt I had seen the hippie's living in communes having free love and I hadn't even tried to live in such a way, boy was there ever a sexual liberation going on alright out there, I just didn't want to be a part of that but I did crave to have a normal life of wife with children to love. However from what I had gone thru my childhood, my life was now going to be on my terms so that for once, I would be the one is at the center of life for those that I want to share life with me. It was during a time of deepest depression & I had a very long time to reflect on who I really am, so when I started coming out of this deepest of deep depressions, I knew I had to seek out gay people to see if they might be able to lead me towards at least a well adjusted state of mind for starters, "Wouldn't that be nice instead of whispering at best for about 1J> yrs. to what was left of my sisters, only 2, my mom dad & grandmother who lived with us, I could always count on her through all of this as granny was now my surrogate mother for life. Since she was literally a Victorian from the 18th. Century, I couldn't bother her with this kind of emotional issue. To do this I feared, more shame & possibly further alienation might have ensued, and that might have finished me off. I also thought that this, to go crazy forever would have made many from this crazy world happy, but I decided to hang on until I might figure out all of these dilemmas out. After I came out of this dismal state of clinical depression then things changed a little for the better.

NEWSFLASH WORLD A BOYFRIEND IS GIVING ME A COMING OUT PARTY

I snuck away to that big city & I was going out on my own to find gay people & ended up at a small famous bar, (we'll call it the OC), where I had heard I'd be welcomed & I was, so I started to meet crazy gay people which wasn't a very good start but from the way I saw it, "much better than crying yourself to death or down to 25 lbs. lighter and I was always the skinny one in the family," no doubt from starvation, I don't have any doubt anyway!

Now I had escaped this trap of my own Mexican American culture that deems it perfectly OK to taunt/harass the hotito's of their own, this mother who bragged that her alliance wasn't to America, that is the USA, but hers was to Mexico. Having escaped in a sense the mindset of this what seemed normal then, & the most crazy behavior of this mothers, in those times, now this behavior that she acted out and allowed others to emulate, I now sought out some kind of normalcy to a battered life, i didn't want others to be allowed to be abusive to me, use put downs often, to treat me badly themselves, but I wanted someone or even a group of people to treat me nicely, with respect and love. For the 1st. time in over a yr. ½ I now have a whole new outlook that I am formulating now I knew that there would never be a period of mourning of all of your childhood that felt like had been stolen, my adolescence which felt like was a joke or a lost time of emptiness that I'd only miss as a time that could have been filled with many beautiful memories, but not the few that I had relished, for one, the pitiful love I derived from a grandmother and that of my best friend, Blackito my little black mongrel buddy. But, to this mom it would seem that I was having too much so probably, she felt she had to intervene. This mother would intervene in the most insidious way imaginable even if you were reading a Steven King novel, this might be more horrible than what you would read in such horror stories.

This way that mother was going to intervene at a time in my life that I finally have found stability with a dear, sweet, same girl that I had dated as a teenager with my dad as chaperone, I now had won back this darling lost love and eventually she becomes my wife but we did get 2 children. This is what this mother decides is what and where she is going to mess with. "At times this hellish mother made me feel like I was a lamb that was being prepared for slaughter, I just didn't know I was being prepared thru this deviant mother's planning to involve my at the time now, common law wife.

SOMETIMES, I FEEL AS IF I AM THE REAL TRUE MYSTERY THAT IS WRAPPED IN AN INIGMA, THIS NATIVE SON THAT GOT TREATED THIS WAY

Mother dearest still was reminding me of her being the mother cat and even though I had left the nest, I was still being reminded by this terrible mother that suffered from the propensity to hurt these children as she reasoned with this old-fashioned thinking, that even at the age of 20, she felt the need to impose her old views on us. Now, realize people that I am now living, working now separated from this terrible nest that sadly I had the misfortune of growing up in, but was about to feel the full force of this terrorist mother's abuse one last time, she must have relished this injury more than all of the aforementioned injuries up to this time. At the very least the mother after she was describing how I was going to have to learn to live with this injury that she was taking full responsibility for. The angriness said it all, as she would tell me that I had to adapt to no longer enjoying sex, her glee and sternness was enough to make me want to kill, but this instead would evolve instead into a brainchild that I had already came up with, and this would say to the world, I have terrorist parentage, but this world seems to think that to torture and abuse and try to kill this sadistic mother's Chicano son was perfectly OK. Now the United States that is to this day still the only country that I've ever known & I still haven't even had a travel Passport ever made as, at the writing of this book time, this is still the case. This unimaginable act that this mother at this age of 20 with her sorry reasoning to the effect that technically since I was not yet the free age of 21, I know was invalid as because I had already moved out and was living with this common law wife, her logic in terms of being Legal was not true, so I would pose it to her but, to no avail, & by now I already knew that there was no point of arguing with this idiot of a mother that fancied herself some kind of supermom, some supermom, more like super-gay son torturer, annihilator and one I never forgot has attempted infanticide. Now I came to the realization after this injury to my penis with a full force kick to it again urged on by this futile mother to not have a homosexual son, sorry, mom you did not destroy this yet, but nice try. Later the name dubbed the come back kid definitely underestimates me as, now all of these abuses come to a head and the creepy mom seems smug and to be quite gleeful about my terrible state of affairs. Aren't you people rooting for her yet, I am a Homosexual even though I am living with my wife that is totally OK with it. This I should interject I enjoyed rubbing into this hellish mother's face.

Needless to say my mother and I my entire life are like vinegar and oil and we absolutely never get along, but what gave this mother the right to injure an adult son that has left the nest and I submit to the entire world, that as always, she would act out her propensity based on probably her girlfriends (probably torture club) on how one treats Hotito's in the Chicano and or Mexican culture/society! I do know for a fact that the Rednecks that are reading these lines as I type them are deliriously happy to hear that I got treated in this way, it's their way too.

My mom apparently still wanted this son to be catatonic, crying himself to death, but did not deserve this girl in this way, what the F was it of her business, and this girl and I were in love in this modern way we were and what business is it of hers, we would still go on and have our beautiful children and make sure that they or these crazy parents never hurt them.

Scientific mother that was a very good clinician still had a notion that I needed to be changed to a girl if I think this way. "Who hasn't heard a child at some point in their lives wish that they were of the opposite gender?" I have, and I don't need to embellish who I heard it from. It was mouthed by me too, when I was developing as a tyke, but never in this tiny little boy's mind would he ever think that this mother could almost have a mantra type of mentality, "I cannot have one single homo or bi-curious child," in this her superchildren brood." For the entire rest of my childhood as I grew up, I always reinforce to this mother that I didn't want to be a girl, yet all that I had was girls in my life as sisters, cousins, aunts, mom & grandmother etc. and the men and boys would always be outside of my life also, they were almost afraid of me as if my effeminate ways that I had learned from all those females might rub off on these very virile men. Actually, they weren't so virile now as I think back, they were full of testosterone for sure though, make no mistake, but, then as time would pass, I naturally would end with much more of this powerful hormone than even my own dad and brother had. Just what the hell do you think that this substance will do to me when this hits my blood? I was told by one sister in particular that I didn't deserve to have the features that developed in me, talk about virile, but I now didn't so much talk like a girl, though I still wasn't able to shake the feminine ways, by now I am very hairy, muscular, and cuter than any boy in the neighborhood and even many of the boys in my very own family. "I guess I really want to say only once, how embarrassing it is to almost self disclose to an immeasurable mass of society about the way that I had actually allowed such a family to break down, that if I had been treated differently and in only good and fair ways this potential superchild that would have outdone all of her precious rest that I was always made to feel inferior to. I never really did ever feel inferior to any of these my siblings just because they had been given a better chance and more advantage than I. Make no mistake people, it is humiliating that this family got to me, and they seem to act as if they know they got away with it. It may be the case that they have, though through the publishing of this book, perhaps they didn't, or won't have.

THIS MOTHER THAT WOULD USE ESTROGEN TO STAY YOUNG AND VITAL MIGHT HAVE THE CAPACITY TO SLIP THIS TO HER FEMININE LIL' BOY

Remember people, this mother who told many people she also was a midwife but not a curandera (Mex. mid wife) had an arsenal of dope of all kinds, some to put one to sleep, some to anesthetize, some to make one feel more like a woman, and who knows, maybe these could be used as her substances to see if a boy that didn't seem to fit in with the rest of the family possibly could be used as her Guiney pig to try to grant his ancient wish of wanting to be a girl. Was my mother slipping this hormone to me my entire life or did she just wait until I was much older, at the age of twenty when I had started talking about the bisexuality in our society & how this was becoming acceptable? Just the same way I was taunted my entire life I also taunted this mother about this & emphasized how now, she had no power over such concepts and I stressed to her that now I was considered emancipated. This statement is the extent of horror that this mother was still willing to instill in her son even after he has come out of practically catatonic state: "We could possibly even still make you a girl you know that was what you asked me for & so you know I'm a good mother & I'm even going to try to give you that!"

All of these terrible things, "the drilling", the crazy mother also still thought of herself as a brainwasher of brainwashers, but I'd tell her this & our fights used to make the foundations of the house tremble! She'd continue, "I don't want this one to grow up & become mean, and aggressive like men do & if he were a girl, he'd be even tempered & milder like our girls, she liked to remind me of this at the tender ages of 7, 8, 9 &10 yrs. old. She'd continue insidiously, "You'd be better off if you were a girl wouldn't you," but you see, I already knew this mother was using reverse psychology, so I'd hate this notion & also, this would be one of her favorite ways to torture and remind me forever of what I had said at 2 yr. or 3 yr. of age, oh, how this torture mother loved her torturing! So, I know many of my readers are going to be interpreting this mother's behavior as clever ploy's and tactics to keep/prevent her son from becoming a dreaded homosexual, but after the childhood torture's inflicted by her on this Native Son from the UNITED STATES OF AMERICA, any current or future taunts will fall on deaf ears, it wasn't about being a homosexual, but there had to be another underlying reason as to why I got treated the way that I did. Let's keep tuned in folks, as I to this day still am searching for the reasons as to why she treated me so terribly. Look for a shocking answer in my part II of this horror true novel that was my life. Others of my little siblings also got punished terribly, but not for their entire lives.

This mother's willingness to actually attempt some kind of sexual transformation of which I didn't want to even hear much less entertain such a thought. Doesn't the thought of this kind of treatment of a son of the 1970's seem absolutely absurd? Well, people, it did to me and it did to my wife I was with too.

From time to time, my mind gets jarred, but one of the very worst child abuses I remember, I didn't care to admit to, "I was just watching an episode of CSI about stark severe child abuse when this reminded me; "I actually got to hear my negotiation as if I were a prostitutible property, but just in the form of an innocent 10 to 12 mo. old, now I know I was barely learning how to speak back & respond with intelligible words but I didn't know what was being proposed was wrong, but it felt creepy & somehow wrong. I was already making mental notes as even though I was full of smiles, this mother had already hurt me and I had already grown to distrust her, do you remember the probing with the long sewing needles to the brain, the Cat Mother didn't have enough food and clothes, diapers etc. for all of her kittens.

At any great length, this uncle was told he could do anything he wanted with me, & I was still in diapers but she assured him I would always be provided to him clean and that I wasn't going to be soiled! In return for this creepy uncle would pay the rent for as long as he stayed & as long as I stayed with him. In essence, I was given to this uncle in lieu of rent pd.! This dreadful mother almost flirtingly told him that he absolutely couldn't hurt me & she made him promise her that I wouldn't be injured such that I might need medical attention, that we (he and she) didn't want to call attn. to their private situation. Then she went on to imply that she was a modern woman & ahead of her time and she was superior to most people's minds, but she had no where else to turn as she was at her wits end in terms of not having the ability to make ends meet so she batted her eyes and even winked at him, and said, pleadingly, "I also assure you that it would be OK, with her & she also would keep mum about this!"

NOW BACK TO THE SELF PROCLAIMED RACIST REBEI'S READING AS I WRITE

I'm hearing many threats as I write this true book, such as, "his alewishious book" he's writing, "who cares about their empty threats of abduction, "aiming at my head right as I sit here at my writing study spot a particular morning a few months ago, but I know full well that these pathetic threats are being designed by thugs in the effort to paralyze me with fear, (not me), never from this (expletive) as I strongly suspect who it and they are, "perhaps they're the same ones responsible for the death of the black girl directly across from that trailer park that I bought in 1989." "A federal raid indeed, why haven't they found the murderer of that girl to date, but I already know that this girl doesn't really matter to their neighborhood, & I'm now the main owner of that entire neighborhood anyway, and I've basically seen that all of these racist haters mostly have been removed from their neighborhood where one has admitted knowing who it was that killed this black neighbor of theirs. You remember, the girl that had a very religious family in that neighborhood, & the one who knew who killed her told me while laughing about it as in the racists in that neighborhood get to get away with it & I ought to know that in the South this is normal & acceptable in 1988 when this happened more or less, as I was told that this is about the time when this terrible murder occurred, just before I bought the small trailer park. "If this were a federal raid, why wouldn't a Federal do something about that horrible murder, but instead continue to call out such as "stupid Mohican, F'n Chicano are heard instead. "Now come on people, I have been to college and I do know better than a group of Federal Raiders would be allowed to treat an American citizen which I am the way that this group of idiots are treating me, if I am the subject of such a Fed. raid, indeed!"

Of this thing be assured, the writing of this book and the reading of it by the public at large is going to get at the bottom of a whole bunch of stuff that is rotten in Denmark.

IN SPITE OF MY MANY DEFECTS NO DOUBT CREATED AT THE HANDS OF THIS BATTERING MOTHER I'M STILL INTACT AND ABLE TO WRITE THIS MYSELF Now, I'm going to go into how I distinctly remember being a perfect child without any of my nervous ticks and many self-doubts and how these self-injuring symptoms came to be so, folks that have still their healthy emotions and souls and hearts intact, get out your tissues and shoulders to cry on as I'll tell you just how a mother can go way to far. Now, get prepared to see just how far a mother that has either been shunned and neglected, or rejected by her loving husband can go to hurt her child?

URGENT NOTICE TO ALL READERS, IF I AM KILLED BY THESE THUGS & RACISTS BEFORE I'M TRU WITH MY REWRITE OF MY BOOK A SON AND SON IN LAW IS GOING TO BE FINISHING THIS REWRITE AS I AM FINISHED

As you might expect, an abusive mother among the Mexican American community is almost unheard of, leastwise, this kind of abuse isn't made publicly known in most cases, so I can't tell you the resistance and lack of encouragement I'm receiving. I really didn't expect that kind of a response, but then I have to interject that the rest of my family has faired well, although they all display similar ticks the same way that I do, only not nearly as severely as I do. Back to my list of injuries at the hand of a mother figure and actual real mother: "My brother's and sisters would have been at the local water reservoir but at the very bottom of it all dressed in their Sunday best clothes, like little angels, was how she put it, had I not strongly discouraged them this one time, & I consider this as one of my worst memories & include as my vivid childhood torture memories as I dearly had grown to love these playmates, we didn't always fight." Back to the crazy Raid by self-proclaimed raiders, and their most recent threat is to aim to shoot and make sure you don't miss, can you just imagine that, me an infamous Mexican American who bought and ran a trailer park in '89 in good old FL. Aside from this I ended up having to work at an international airport and also additionally to those 2 jobs, I also had to be a caregiver by of helping an older senior to eat, walk, to to the doctor, and yet keep this Park going while surrounded by pure Racists hurling accusations ad-infinitum. Still, this was somewhat becoming a life which seemed fill of mediocrity to me! The only thing I care that happens to these nuisance Raiders who stalk and are hold up in the adjacent apt. is that, they end up truly reading this and find out how their antics are not what led up to my writing this book. I know that if these regarded outlaws by our Govt. just go away with the knowledge that I at least had the compassion to not inform the (he or they just called out fagot) news media and other Federal authorities of the things that these creeps managed to spill out of their mouths, their slips of their tongues. When these outlaws are gone and out of my life, then, I won't tell how I know by way of these idiots telling me that they have knowledge of a Black teen girl who was murdered directly in the vicinity of this trailer park that I bought in 89'. These sort ought to know better than to be fooling with someone like me who's as mad about this fact as I am, but nobody else in this neighborhood cares about this girl.

Enough with these infidel and subversive dissidents, and back to the main topic, subject, and the germane issue where I was: The description of my many injuries that affected my life forever! I hate when I'm acting like when I was in that horrible cell/dirt pit, that became my home for many months from which I would only be found no doubt to my window shattering screams, someone most have heard me! I remember vividly having-gotten horse when my mother would come to feed me by way of throwing gnawed bones at me. My sisters always like to remind me of when I was a teen & we'd play practical jokes on one another, how I one time tinkled in a Mt. Pew bottle and told them it was great drink, anyway, two of these teasing sisters partook so in this way, I got back at them for when I always had to eat off their gnawed bones and I had to do this because I had nothing else at all to eat, "and they think they ingested my germs!" I do hope they read this book so they might know that we should all be all OK with one another. I think we all got our paybacks in before we all left that terrible nest. so as this little child I had to come to grips that I might die in this pit, as this mother had finally gone haywire, and I already looked at her whenever she'd show herself because she had to bother to come and hurl those gnawed bones at me like she was some kind of psycho, which she had now become, no one should treat a child of any age the way that I was being treated, and she did get away with this.

I developed the squirming mannerisms that I still live with today, OCD, when I was locked up in this cell & I was constantly being reminded that I was bad, worthless, useless, a burden, that I needed to be eliminated more than just being kept in this pit as I was the eating machine of the family & the rest of the precious weren't going to be the ones that were going to go without, but I was.

Anyway, had I not squirmed constantly, I developed something like bed sores & when I'd complain to this mother, then she would be more accurate when she threw these useless bones that were so sharp that at times they'd hit me and cut my skin which made her laugh and gleeful. I think she had Redneck in her and the fact is that there was a Texan that boinked my grandmother's mom that was the way that that of the side of the family got so albino white. Did that great grandmother bring meanness of the white people into our family, this is true and mom used to tell of how her grandmother was a maid for this rancher and that was when my grandmother was made. I talked to this grandmother, and she confirmed that she did not know who her father was, so I feel from knowing my family's history that this is when this family's blood was infected with this man's blood, the blood of hatemonger's of the Red neck's propensity and typical behavior. Now, why do I have to suffer because this grandmother had no father that she knew, and the only one that was pinpointed by way of family lore was this Redneck from Texas who had his way with his housekeeper? It's utterly ridiculous that my injuries were being inflicted due to the drop of Redneck blood in her, I know this, but get these monkeys off my back, because if they're not removed, this book is going to remove this threat that they think is over my head, again I say, they are nothing but nuisances and a futile waste of time but their time will be redirected to investigating the murder of that black Christian girl that surely was murdered by one of their own of that neighborhood, and they have to continue suppressing this information to save someone's ass in that hole of a so called hollow.

Apparently, these idiots who are set up next door and sound every-bit like pure red necks, must have been aiming at my head and I mean aiming to kill as I have just heard them proclaim that, "I should have shot him before when I could have recently, he would have been mine," now readers what do you think, will I get to finish rewriting this book in double space, formatted, and proofread, or do you think my son in law and or son are going to have to finish the rewrite of this so that it is acceptable for a publishing house.

This squirming that I exhibit from time to time, goes back to the cell and dirt floor not high enough to stand up even for me a tyke, it was very hard to get comfortable in that pit, and I knew that if I didn't fidget at all I ended up with bedsores, only with dirt floor for a bed, these were actually dirt bed sores, and I so still remember having to adjust positions constantly to avoid getting severely dirt bed sored, so this just one of the ways that I will learn to survive. Then there was when I developed the child version of complete and utter hybernation, and this is the only way that I had devised to conserve what little energy that I was able to save for when she would horribly come to the trap door to inflict psychological and physical injuries to me an infant that should have been in the hands of a caregiver that was not so inclined/bent at torture and abuse! You would be surprised how an infant will fight to live, now there is another trick that I learned in that pit so that I could outwit this mother that it now became clear to me that it didn't matter whether I lived or died. I learned to gnaw the cartilage at the ends of the bones that I managed to catch as her game also was you don't catch, "and this vicious mother would look at this helpless innocent child with a look that said, now just see if you are going to miss catching these morsels that I was supposed to be considering regarding such a way, but these just like to Jesus, were mere dirty rags to me, though I'm not implying that I was anything like our Jesus! Not to sound stupid, but I probably would have fared better had I learned to break the bones and suck out the marrow. I already knew, and I wasn't stupid, that those juicy morsels that she was referring to weren't these terribly gnawed bones, but the morsels she was referring used to be morsels, and my siblings were the ones that got to enjoy them as the morsels they used to be.

I literally saw life slip away as I heard cheer, glee, satiation from a good real meal just above me from my other brother and sisters/ then I'd hear dead silence so I knew that these little selfish self serving siblings had fallen into a dead slumber from fullness. Oh well, at least I didn't have to hear them frolicking about above at the brick school house while I was locked up i horrible prison pit of my mothers design.

A resounding AHHHHH these horrific days are over except the memories that I have to revisit in the writing of these terrible memories & or you could say nightmarish toddler memories I somehow have survived but the constant Redneck braggarts love nothing more than to act like the bully that my mother was, they totally remind of this behavior of hers. Now folks, you can imagine how I am not going to be bullied by functional illiterates of this sort of magnitude, they're bullies to the point of absurdity the very same way that this bitch of a mother was.

They actually think that they can get to me and aren't going relent until they do, as they know that I have had a history of nervous breakdowns. Their raid is for a whole lifetime they like to brag, but, this I do know better, as they're all corrupt, and I am totally on the good side of the law and am not involved with the cover up of the murder of a neighbor a stone's throw from it. I say it, because these aren't good or great Red Necks which I respect, but they're the jailbird variety, so I am not intimidated by them, rest assured.

If the people reading this story are doubtful about the dangerousness of this FL, self proclaimed red neck neighborhood, just let me tell you that I grew up with game hunter's as a child, my brother and my dad were both avid hunters. I learned from that the way that a bullet sounds when it is flying thru the air, and I know that the sound resembles that of a huge pyrotechnic, fire-cracker or holiday rockets that are launched into the sky for brilliant sky displays, and I literally felt them fly right by my head, along with the sound that they make, I actually felt something like warmth then as they hurled by me, then they'd make a dying out sound as they reached their end point like in the valley area that was the end of my property! I think these local yokels were actually trying to kill the new owners of this trailer trash trailer park that we had bought! They were doing this I suspect due to the fact that they had previously gotten away with killing the black girl I so often refer to, and this girl is begging thru her unrested soul thru me to find the murders of her life and bring these villains to account and be held responsible for her death. What possible good is it going to do these scoundrels to raid me until the end of my life? This won't bring this girl back to life, but maybe the writing of this book will open up this sorry and sordid case of a community gone wrong when a neighbor that I was told they used to ride the bus to school with is killed in cold blood right in their very own midst. According to one neighbor who I know and lives in that mess still, the only ones that do care about her were only her own Nigger family as I was told! Sorry I had to use that N word, but as you can guess, I do not mean this in a put down way, just read the context that it's in.

Now I hope that this will shed some light on this period of my child incarceration, "of my precious fedora with a feather," for all the time that I was in that hole, about 3 or 4 months, for having had to endure this worse than enslavement time lost forever, I receive an almost only time gift of a fedora with a feather in it. Once I had seen it in a store so I told mom I liked it but this must cost her a lot. She told me that this hat would make me feel better, and I got resented by my brothers and sisters, they were totally like her, self centered, overly competitive, self-serving, bullish etc., so this sort of scared me & I offered it to one or two of them but for once, she was to tell them that this hat would only be reserved for me and only me. Because I knew that this mom wanted me to be happy with this, I knew that I had to act like I was consoled, so that was what I did, what would you do? I was still in shock though so I knew that I just had to be one of her little goose stepping little tin soldiers as she loved to regard us when we'd obey this torture mother blindly. I from the extreme confinement/isolation, knew, though in shock that I pretty much better do most of her bidding the same way that her other children were doing, though I still was not going to be led to the eating of feces! By the way, I despised the way these toy soldier siblings kissed this mother's ass to gain favors!

This tender time of my formative life is when I stopped being the baby in the family (I was the youngest) still I was going to have to learn to be just like the rest or risk the same treatment that I had gotten before, never mind what this creature had told the policewoman/social worker, she immediately would go back to status quo of child drilling to the point of abnauseum, and deprivation, and favoritism. Everything that was promised in my presence to this official was her carefully constructed lie as she had ill regard for these authorities and I knew that I was living under a monster in the disguise of a sorry excuse of a mother. I remembered how not a one of my siblings were even a little concerned while I lived in a pit, because they themselves would have an awful lot to eat, though after I got out they looked at me like they were happy that this hadn't happened to them or to the one that she had selected to go into this pit so that this would save plenty enough food for the momma cat's rest of her litter that were strong and reliable for doing her bidding. Yet, still, these co-siblings displayed many of the mannerisms of this mother, especially her smugness and haughtiness.

If this was truly my biological mother she did nothing but belittle and degrade, humiliate and heap condemnation and scorn for almost the entire time of my life that I was raised under her.

Recently a very nice brother in law sent me a picture of me standing along all of the 4 other siblings & mom just after I had gotten saved from this horrible pit, and I still was suffering from the effects of starvation, nicks/cuts from bone-throwing, trembling that is almost gone but not yet completely. He didn't know this, or else, I don't think that he would have sent this. I look like a child that has been starved of affection from being in an orphanage, I'm facially drawn, I even have an expression of shock as I am thinking what in the hell do I want to pictured with these crazy mindless elders who don't know better than to eat shit when this mother asks to do so. Not only do I look extremely un-health, but I also look like a child that happens to also be a war victim. Yet, like some little monkey that I knew that I had to be, I had this abzurcl stupid looking hat on, with a feather!

Nevertheless in the picture I cried a lot & had to demand that I be included & finally after much pleading I had to do also, she agrees to allow me to be included in this family picture. Now as I reflect I realize that as unhealthy as I look and knowing how smart I was, she had reasons to not want me to be included in that picture, just look at how this brought back a cascade of bad memories! In this pathetic picture that for me documents the terrible way that I was put in a dungeon, "I look very small & strained because I was recovering from the shock & the starvation just subjected to but this mom's plan was to continue with the sabotaging of my childhood. I guess she had me by making me beg to be included as the others also agreed that I shouldn't be included in it. This hateful mother told the others that I was too ugly to be in our, their family picture even after all that torture, she was still up for more administering psychological torture, these authorities weren't going to tell her what to do. This mother would say to the others, "He's too ugly, and ask, "do you all really want him to be connected with the rest of all of you beautiful children?" This was true as I was suffering from malnutrition that I hadn't recovered from yet. Still, I didn't deserve to have my pic taken with the others because I'd ruin the picture as they were all plump, not mal but over nourished and if I get this picture again, I'll include it in this book as an illustration so you will believe this. I also really believe that the hat was bought mainly to cover up the gash that this mother had inflicted to my skull! The hat served a multipurpose for my mother that had too many kids that she couldn't afford she had complained. From this gash she administered, to this day I can't grow hair & it's hard to cover up, and this messes with my avant-garde look that I'm sometimes trying to cultivate, ha ha. All of these memories came to me the minute I 1st saw that picture I so vividly remember.

I do love my siblings as I write this at the age of 58, but this sister made me mad that she would have so easily forgotten, what memory that this picture would have triggered. In fact, I cried out loud because the freshly healed would might as well have had salt poured on it by this co-sibling to send this pic' to me in the mail! I'm starting to wonder if this sister is trying to take the torturer's place, I should have not offered to go in her place instead, she should have been the one in there for months.

REFLECTIONS OF A TORMENTED PAST FOR A BOOK IS NECESSARY FOR THIS TO COME TO PRINT, BUT MY VOW IS TO NEVER ALLOW IT TO RUN MY LIFE

Go ahead and be jealous if you want if my book is super-cussful due to the horrors that were real and true, but, this isn't the goal of my story, as I learned in life that to be unnecessarily proud over such things, even the sense of a getting back have the potential of ruining a persons soul. The very purpose for which I do write this book, (to sensitize and re-humanize humanity,)to make them see and feel what effects may come from such treatment of a soul that is innocent and like an empty vessel which depending on what is put into the vessel, does take shape to what is put into this vessel.

I truly know from actual life experience what it means to yearn just to walk about freely & be treated at least as good as our dogs which ate better left over's & dog food so I just had to let the days wane as I dreamed & prayed to some yet unknown GOD that I might be saved from this miniature dungeon at about 2 yrs. old as my problem from what I could gather was that I ate too much & I didn't listen after I had also heard my mom declare that she had the power to make me into whatever she chose so now to support her hatred of me further & so that I could suffer all my life she had changed her mind & decided to make me into a (hotito or maricone) & so that's probably when she also decided it would be better to change me into a girl(literally)! This was based on what a child (me) that doesn't yet know better than to ask for such a thing had asked for, yes, I had asked for "such a thing", "can I be a girl, "it's really what I want to be," to a horrified mother that possessed excellent medical background, this mother actually believed she could pull off making the switch, what a megalomaniac mother! "She reminded me about this most of my life because she knew this was a great shame tactic so this of course from the way she acted, to say this to a little tyke made this mother feel better than me, she would even say as much to me. She was without any doubt, above me and better than me, and as the wise all-knowing parent she was determined that she was going to be steering me right, "I don't think so." But I made it a point not to listen to this mother, for example, many of the times I would be placed against my will in areas I didn't want to be or I couldn't move because the mother would tie me up when I was asleep as GOD knows I had become (rabid) after needles in the head, meat cleaver to the head, tourniquet around my penis and balls, you bet I'm not going to listen to that crazy mother because who are you, because you don't act loving anymore like my mother used to who started out this way. This looked like the same mother except the twisted look of hatred grimace on the monster's face, and now all that this mother can do is, "apply more tightening to the tourniquet," "you said you wished you could become a girl & I just wanted to make that wish come true, see I am a good mommy!"

Just after the testicals turned purple to almost black little sister peeked in to see what she was up to as she knew that this was going on, why else would she have had this terrified worried look on her face that haunts me still sometimes when I look into this still living sister's eyes? I guess I owe to this other siblings a bit of gratitude for getting to keep these my family jewels, ha!

At any rate, the mother was about to pull on the tourniquet when little sister says, "don't do that, it doesn't look ready, but this mother looked like she was in so much of a hurry, that I'm almost totally sure that she would have gone thru with this most horrible of horrible tortures, (this in fact would've been a most vicious of physical mutilations to date) at her hands that she would have committed to date! For some reason, this didn't seem to phase her as she seemed so psyched by something, that this fervor that she was displaying seemed to be coming from it seemed to me like from some kind of injury that she had sustained that she was now preparing to inflict upon me, someone that should have been considered her loving son. I knew by now though that I was far from this. I often asked her, this person that was supposed to represent my mother, are you really my mother, because you don't act anything like the mother I knew! I thought, you sure don't act like you even like your son much less like you love me, your little helpless and developing battered son! So little sister stopped her from pulling on the contraption that she had wrapped around my penis and testicles, the tightening of her clamp she thought prematurely was now ready for her ultimate surgical procedure, the time had come to convert her falsettoish son's gonads! The falsetto came from being around nothing but girls and as you have read, I was constantly scolded if I used any of the lower octaves of my little boy's voice.

Now that I'm older and I reflect upon that time when I was so clinically depressed and my interminable crying that eventually would come to an end. What was the thing that I was mourning the most, the way that I had allowed others to injure my genitals thru their underhanded trickery and plotting and conspiring against me as well. I was now after this final physical abuse so physically diminished and reduced that this alone became the single most resented aspect of my treatment by this family that treated me so terribly for the most part of my upbringing in that setting, my siblings, were allowed to say things like, "We took a vote, and you are going to be neutralized because you have too out of control of a sex drive, the vote was not in your favor," I was told the vote was among the three sisters and this torture mother that was permitted to raise me for what is still some unexplainable reason to me! She was nothing but a torture mother to this child! And at a very late stage in my 20th yr. of age already, what business did these sisters have in determining a vote to perform an illegal surgical abuse on a sibling that is not even living at home and in the house of this torture mother's anymore. One mean sister who was regarded one of the champions in terms of vicious the way you had to become to survive in this family could say to me, "I always thought you didn't deserve what you had between your legs and I'm the strong one but instead you got that, but I still am with mom and we're going to fix that problem you have with that thing between your legs." This is the way that my so called elder's were allowed to speak to me by the mother that bragged to me also that she was still capable of being the cat and even though I had left the nest I wasn't yet of age. AND NEWSFLASH, AS I JUST WENT TO RESUME THE WRITING OF THIS HORRIFIC OF HORROR TRUE AMERICAN STORIES, when surprise of surprises, my rough draft is gone! I know the readers may be wondering how in the heck am I going to be able to finish such a horrible story when this rough draft has showed up missing and the ones claiming to have snatched are, you guessed it, the Raiders who have vowed to ruin my life! I guess you know by now who these culprits might be and of course they are bragging on how they are able to raid me at any time and for anything of mine that they want. Yes, the Raiders are claiming having snatched my rough draft in the hopes that I would then not be able to finish this book. The fallacy with this reasoning of theirs is that this is based on my real life plight and I have all of this information permanently engraved in my brain matter, so this small loss is of no consequence to me, only merely a tiny inconvenience. These malfeasants never fail to input such behaviors as this which only is serving to make this my life story even more interesting and unputdownable to any suspense reader. I've taken a 3 week break from this writing and this actually gives me a fresh new outlook plus one more thing to tell on these hold up Raiders that are hold up next door in a hate cell group as to have stolen this or claimed to have stole this draft from me only thickens the plot of my novel. Let's give a communal thank you to the Raiders to be making this story even more interesting that it would have been.

DEPRAVED REGARD FOR LIFE LIKE THE RAIDERS CLAIM TO HAVE ACTED OUT

Voluntarily induced abortions brought on thru illegal methods as seen recently on an SVU episode were things my mom was thoroughly capable of performing and I wouldn't even of put it past her to have caused her own! This mother committed such abuses on me that I wouldn't have put anything past her.

Thru the writing of this novel and auto bio', I sure hope to impact our government with regards to such injured persons as I was. It is my earnest hope that I might be able to found a number of Organizations to benefit such forgotten individuals with potentially dynamic potential as I may possess. Even though people can be experiencing emotional breakdown, such people can and will still strive to achieve some sort of sense to their lives as they can't say the hell with this world when they might be experiencing downward turns either psychologically or emotionally. In the words of one of my sister's best black friends, "You can't say the hell with society when you have to live in and with it." Sadly, her name has to go unmentioned.

DEPRAVED REGARD FOR LIFE: ASSISTED SELF INDUCED ABORTION

In my next volume I'll talk about an induced abortion that was committed in the late 60's with my mother as the one who provided the agent that would induce abortion. This was one of her Florence Nightingale sorry efforts to fix a helpless girl that due to a rogue boyfriend had gotten in trouble. I do know that this did not fix this girls life by having talked with her about this and she admitted to me also that now she would have to learn to live with this. Much of my mother's behavior as you could guest as absolutely appalling to me and bordered on the incomprehensible. Like the time mom taught me that whenever you play with the reproduction area of a bug or the gonad area of let's say a frog, they'll come out fighting almost as if psychotically, wouldn't you, well, anyway that once was a choice that I didn't even have and I remember on two occasions that she tried this to me her 1 yr. old and again when I was probably 2! I call this depraved regard for life alright & I was the one at the end of the knife she and my dad were holding as they contemplated their actions. Boy, this is one time that I learned to talk fast before they'd ruin my life forever. At the first attempt the mother was trying to persuade the father that I probably was a threat to the girls and probably I would have been better off without this appendage and two testicals and as the father listened intently, instead he thankfully would prefer my reasoning of hey, ain't I your little boy you said you love anymore, don't you even try to use that to do that to me, so dad didn't the villainous act but he might have been drunk at the time. That he might have been drunk meant that he very well could have carried it out! Sadly, mom knew that her husband was an illiterate brute and was thoroughly capable of doing this to a threat to his masculinity. When my dad would tie on a drunk, obviously the illiterate felt that he was omnipotent. Sin embargo, they would have both gone to jail. Just the same horrible way that she would urge on my other siblings, mom would say things to my dad at that terrible moment, "Just look at those huge cahones, do they even look like they're even bigger than yours?" Not a good thing to say to a Mexican male if he's in his prime like my dad was at the time, so I would then get this terrified look on my face and I knew that I had to learn to talk fast, now, what do you think about that?

I did have an unusually large set of Cahones for being just a little tyke of 2 or 3 & let there be no mistake, I was happy with them then, and now when I look back, today I can say that I am proud to have had them huge when I already just had the instinct that those were there for a reason. I also do remember hearing my dad argue in their defense saying that those were also part of his little boy's beauty, what a dad! Sin embargo, "nonetheless", I was still sweating it out, and I still had that psychotic mother coaxing him on with, "just look at his behavior already and I think that it's because he has those and they are causing him to act out much more aggressively than any of the others ever have, & it now Santos, don't you have to agree with me?

While this may have been true that I had acted out more aggressively than any of the others ever had, but then, I had never seen them have to fight for their lives the way that I had been made to & I still don't understand why the mother who definitely possessed the valiant potential to strike her own child with a meat cleaver still was allowed to be involved with raising these children that also displayed signs of child abuse. And so now in such a tone, I have to begin to wind this portion of my novel down as I reiterate, my files were broken into so my rough draft was either stolen, or this constant Raiding me has caused me to forget where I have placed it, but, I'll type one last brainstorm that wasn't with the last of this rough draft, but let me add that this rough draft was written in my own personal code so that no one else would be able to transcribe but me, so this is the only copy that Is accurate and complete, then I'll furnish a forward and an afterword.

This Book Could Be Considered Also Julian's Letter From The Hole

I still have to say to this world that by doing this that was done to me, that of allowing such a torture mother to continue to torture this her very own child so grotesquely might have been a portent of what was to come or was it of what this twisted mother that was capable of such tortures was devising and engineering to scare the world to death, now, after all that I have written, try to make any sense of it! Consider that I just may well be a hero of modern kind who thru his own revisional memories figured out the solution to his own problems & completely without the help of any kind of professional assistance. The memories that I have herein written about are true to best of my knowledge and I will not include anything that wasn't absolutely real and true memories that I strove all of my life to forget, which would have left very few good memories. As I went thru life I tried with all my might to create good memories to replace these terrible ones and I managed to succeed somewhat, but these terrible flashbacks always seemed to ruin any friends that I might make or any sort of stability that I might try to make my life into along with two beautiful children and a hotter than hot wife! What did this family care about this bi-sexualis son as I was claiming to be so as not to appear as not being true to myself. That was a phase I felt also coerced into like the famous proverb about leading a horse to water but you can't make him drink. My fragile state I now know after all these years was obviously brought on by pier pressure and by a domineering mother who went to her grave with that scowl on her face that I would make when I was disgruntled, wow was I ever amazed. I thought, "why does this mother have the very look that I so felt when all of the ills of the world would visit me or in other words, when everything went wrong." This is the very scowl and facial expression that this deceit mother displayed to the world from her miserable caufjin now I knew that I could finally lay my co-hatred to rest with this pitiful excuse for a mother that I had to endure for all of the formative part of my life and I sure have to admit that I definitely didn't want to be anything like this mother and I sure hope that I'm not anything like her to my children or to the world.

As to the up in arms neighborhood of self proclaimed racists who were ever so willing to excuse my behavior as just typical ill fag behavior but I actually even did manage to get some input from these neighbors that were indications of understanding but being the ill behavior that was being exhibited several warnings had been made. But there were no warnings being made to these admitted criminals with proud records about the dead teenaged black girl that had been murdered a stone's throw from my front yard. I call that ill behavior indeed. Nothing was being said about ill behavior such as bragging to me about this murder and boasting also of knowing the person that committed the murder & telling it with a smug proudness of having gotten away with it. I also call this typical ill non fag Red Rebel Raider behavior!

MY PSYCHODELLIC TRIP WAS EDGAR ALLAN POESQUE How would you like somebody to slip you an illegal substance without your knowledge when you are experiencing these type of psychosis's already that have been mentioned in this book? Try Crystal meth & or Ecstasy of a designer drug variety, how would that suit you? When I went to buy an aphrodisiac that I liked & I bought it, I later found out that the very brand and the batch sold in the local area had been tampered with the abovementioned illegal narcotics. Sin embargo, I liked it so I went back and checked to see if there were any more that looked liked they had been opened and tampered with the way the one that made me have trip like response had. Sure enough there was 2 or so & boy was I in for the ride of my life, I would end up giving a new meaning to the title "The Naked Civil Servant", yet I would have just the same have been the town crier & wigged out Naked Civil Servant. I also was angry and crying about an entrapment arrest, & at the same time, I had not been marandized nor was I ever marandized yet I was arrested which was violation of my constitutional rights as a U.S. citizen & I was tripping and angry about many of these issues & having to work 3 jobs to pay $1000's of dollars of taxes only to drive used cars! Many things had me mad while I came undone & even more undone under this unknown illegal substance. Try to bear in mind that I have also the vow to this mother that when my life goes awry she'll be the sorry one & so I also had vowed to her that since she had wanted my sex to be ruined then, instead this sex of mine was going to be the ruination of her and her precious worship of money and power world! "Fuck you, you whore, you prostitute to your torture god & god you cunt", I'd call out yelling while I was on this rage trip, can you imagine such behavior, well, now this seems so strange to me & it should. Remember, I now have a stable life and am writing this my true life story as the basis for a titillating horror story as that is just about what this horror life story amounted to. Getting back to this trip, I wanted to flash to avenge the torture mother that this system made me have to suffer, In her honor the torturess of the Rodriguez kids who must have worshiped some torture deity! It felt like it was all I could do not to buy a gun and kill something or someone even myself, but yet I had children that I wanted to do good for and amass some wealth to share with them. I felt that I totally was being watched so I felt that since I was under the floodlights, I may as well put on a good show & this ought to be spectacular, I was under the big lights now! The stage was all mine & I had a captive audience now, more fuel to my fire. I was being as promiscuous as I could possibly be so as to ruin this sweet innocent person that I was wanting to be to ruin that image for my mother & now I wanted total self destruction, so I would go to every man I could get my hands on and as many times as I could, so there hellish mother, your son is a total true libertine and not as injured as you thought, fucking bitch. Remember folks, I'm trippin on unknown substance bought at a convenience store, so I wanted to pay back this torrid world that did this to its native son, me more so & stronger than ever in my life so I would set out to try to ruin a life or at least adversely affect it to make it feel the way I had been made to feel & yes that would include inferior although I never did succumb to this feeling completely. This is now my self inflicting torture method that I have devised since my mother had not wanted me to live my fragile mind would reason. So becomes the fragile mind of an emotionally disturbed tripper, it becomes even more fragile.

All the time that I was behaving in this so very horrible way I was remembering all the time that I was in the horrible pit that this torture mother who was supposedly also my biological mother had devised. I was also contemplating what this horrible neighborhood that I had bought into was treating me the same way that they talked about the murdered girl was treated, is the same way that these Racist Raiders were certainly making sure that I would be treated. I could have been their next murder victim in that neighborhood since I wasn't an Anglo white American I was told. It didn't matter that I & my business partner had the largest land holdings in the immediate area, we were also fags to these so called neighbors & I was directly responsible for one of these people's son to obtain a check and medicine for his health problem which was ADD but, remember I still was just a fag to his father who almost always was my worse adversary in this burg of which I own the most housing and property.

Today is 9.11.11 and I as much as I hate to admit this, last night I had such horrible nightmares with regard to this torture mother that I know that its because the rough manuscript that I was using to write this book was misplaced or stolen. This I already planned to have finished but these cretins who follow me around interminably and are always warning me that are going to be doing this until I stop the writing of this book which is also my true life story, this is why I don't buy that I misplaced it but I've only heard brag about 2 million times that they have gotten this out of my very hands & this is supposed to be a great achievement for this so called Raider's espionage effort. So how is this going to help them with all of the potentially demanding evidence mentioned about them and their precious hate neighborhood? How is this going to help them when I still have all the terrible memories in my head3 from my entire life & including the horrific so called memories that were made while living in this excuse of a neighborhood? I came to these hate mongers like the lamb I was to my mother & they certainly rejoiced that I was a Gay so that they could taunt and heckle and defile whenever they could have a chance, but these cretins didn't count on one of the fags planning to amass a stronghold of satellite properties besides this miserable trailer park which would guarantee us continual rent so that no amount of rent strikes would destroy us or our attempts of our net worth growth, ha!

Nevertheless, getting back to the dream that was more a nightmare in which this hate mother hadn't even touch her son for several months and this made me cry and yell this to her, "why won't you touch me and love me anymore?" She was all wrinkled & I surmise that in my dreams of her I want to paint her as weak & withered & I suppose subconsciously I view her as weak & withered compared to me as I did overcome this hate mothers abuses by totally leaving her vicinity just like I know that she wanted and to this day I still have never moved back. I vowed that I would never go back to being treated in the ways that she would treat me & I never have. That hate mother would die with a scowl on her face exactly like the one I displayed whenever she would prod me to act out horribly the way that I felt compelled to act out.

I know you ask as readers, are curious and probably titillated by reading the sorry torments by this horrid torture mum, how could a mother induce a son to behave in such a totally aberrant and torrid manner & I will tell you. This mother knew of this behavior and in a way this mother was my accomplish to this terrible behavior. My very own mom who is much the subject of this book could say such things as, "I told you that since you aren't one of the other children that have embraced Catholicism version of Christianity, I have to not care about your actions & anything that you do is only on you, & she'd pipe in one of my famous axioms that she learned from sort of being my soul mate, "I can't control you any more as you know, you are in control of your own nerve endings aren't you now, so beware of the rest Of the good ones as they too aren't happy with your behavior," now I knew that this mother was still bent on ruination of anything I do, so she even set out to meet some of the neighbors in this neighborhood that I had bought into with my life-mate at the time. From what I gathered from the surrounding neighbors, none of them wanted anything to do with meeting any relative of mine, & this is when my mother realized that I was again living in a neighborhood that had it infer the sub groups that I and my partner were associated with. One criminal that lived in this area told me that if a person looked into the eyes of their potential victim then they would never be able to injure this person & or kill them and this is what he had learned in one of the many stays that he had spent in prison and from his inmates. Needless to say, since I knew that this creep was this way, I accompanied this mother & father who were snubbed by him in keeping with his philosophy of not looking into any people perceived to be as enemies or threats to his plan to take over the neighborhood ultimately, and believe it or not folks, even if this person is in jail, I still believe that this same person is conducting illegal raids with the help of such wealthy R'Necks who on multiple trailer parks in the neighboring town. He used the reasoning that they were the only white ones who should own trailer parks so that these vast owners of hundreds of units would take his side and fund undermining me thru raids of my services to my small park & eventually the surrounding properties that I and my associate had amassed.

The joke of this to me is that both of these people represented creepy behavior to me, he is the lowliest of people selling dope, stealing cars, verbally assaulting minorities and Gay business people, and she was my child torturer and physical abuser unlike any had abused me even surpassing my brute teenage brother who was directed to injure my arm every chance he could so that I might become tough she would say to him, & then she would add that this would build much muscle that he needed to develop, as this brother was the biggest school jock at our school anyway.

This brother who was directed to inflict injuries on a child 8 yrs. younger did this happily as he hated this little hotito, (queer) little brother & he had grown fond of being a bully to me his little brother. After all, this saintly mother had sanctioned such sub-human behavior as appropriate and deserving so I eventually developed a hate for this older only other male in the family besides dad, and he was just a drunken oaf to me much of the time.

Yes folks, on this memorial day of 9.11, I woke up with that evilest of evil mothers being at the center of my most terrible of terrible nightmares. "Why don't you love me anymore I cried out vainly as in my entire remainder of my life I would never be loved the way that any child out of necessity should be loved, with the touch of your nurturing mother and with plenty of touch, with plenty of affection and kind words with reassurance and fondness, but not with the hatred that this mother demonstrated and with traumatizing hostility like I had never known and to this day I still haven't known such abusive behavior such as this mother committed on me. I experienced my own personal 9/11 when I was literally a toddler with my very own demented mother & on this holy day of memory, I also mourn the loss of my childhood based on who knows what, & I guess I would have to revive the long dead to see if this hideous mother might able to shed light on the topic.

I do know myself and I know that now I'll probably forever link today's 10 yr. remembrance of this 9/11 nightmarish American tragedy with my own, & I actually believe that they do compare. At the time of my toddler years, I am already experiencing a death of my ID as just as I start to form a sass of who I am, the pokes thru my skull in her probing way has already happened. Though this day will be also linked with this nightmare I had on the memorial day, if I am writing this account today, I can assure everyone reading this, I won't let these flashbacks ruin me and knowing that it is all in the past & that I'm just writing about these events to put this hoar memories to rest.

I don't like talking this way about real true horrible memories as if I liked titillating the way I'm suggesting as I write, yet, the way our society enjoys seeing humans suffer the way they depict them going thru this, it is such a trend that I apologize if I suggest that everyone will feel that these torture experiences are loved by all readers. I know that there's many readers who are going to understand how a parent could go haywire & purported to be like a demigod and know all omnipotent sort of ogre to tiny developing infants. It was my misfortune and the rest of the world's that I had to be the one that was in this mother's way. This was my very own child torturer 9/11 10 yr. memorial nightmare mother!

THE 9/11 TORTURE NIGHTMARE 10 yr. MEMORIAL INFANTICIDAL MATRIARCH PIT/DUNGEON FOOD THROWER IS MY LEADER TO SEVERAL PITS

The 1st pit, was the one as the 2 to 3 yr. old, the second pit is when I go thru puberty at 12 and I'm cast to a century old basement full of black widows, dampness, coldness, and my third pit was when I had the room upstairs that I virtually didn't leave for over a year as I experienced a terrible identity crisis & this sickening mother would taunt, "would you still like to become a girl, as I might be able to assist you so that you can finally get your wish, can you believe that? The truth of the matter is I most of the times end up feeling as if I am burning my own ears by having to hear myself think these terrible lines but, it's what this story is about and I have to remember it to write the horror childhood that I endured. That is why I didn't want to lose this rough draft because I had already lived thru it again to write that, but now if these outsiders have obtained this draft, I know they'll twist it & try to depict me like some kind of subversive or radical, & I'm actually one of the most pacifistic people you would ever meet. Already, I've heard some of the taunts from this excuse of a mother being used by those voices that keep making the claim that they're in control of my life, & I'm under their Red house arrest, How absurd, there is no Red arrest that wouldn't ball lowed in the U.S. Any so called arrest would definitely constitute an illegal arrest. $_{wit}$h total violation of my constitutional rights. At the time that I was upstairs deteriorating away emotionally just a ball of nerves, I credit this mother to having driven me there although she had made as though she was wanting to be a mother finally^ but I just knew that I had to try to cling on to some kind of sanity though sometimes I just felt like I was so slipping away that soon there might be a point of no return. In all honesty, I think to be acting this way this mother must have figured out how to slip me her estrogen pills that she had bragged to us about that her very good Dr. prescribed to her to stave off her menopause & she also liked to add that this made her much more feminine and stronger & would also help to keep her young. Still the selfish self-serving mother at the expense of the loser son, that would never cost her or my dad a cent, and this was their bond & I had heard them agree to this oath of theirs, so I also feel that this was just another way to deny me any semblance or any sense of normalcy to this child's development. I guess this sort of makes my dad her partner in child crime but I just kept feeling left out and not equal to the rest of my siblings.

These siblings who witnessed this child torture were even made to be child torturers themselves whose names I can't disclose who were also no doubt her victims also. Yes mom, they do always want to place blame on the mother, Sin embargo, in this case they should have. These grotesque injuries I endured s and survived should have been dismissed just so easily is the way that she regarded these matters & so she'd point out that thinking this way was a sign of my weakness & if anything I should be thankful that she cared enough to try to toughen me up. To me now, this seems like a manly way to act for a mother who is supposed to be demonstrative to little babies, anyway, at one time in my childhood this fickle mother did act in loving ways to all of us I clearly remember this much. Again I have to digress, just the same way she'd (mom) say, "you shouldn't have done it in the first place,[1] I think she shouldn't have teased me when I was the tiniest tyke with these loving ways that she displayed & are my real true earliest memories.

WHAT WOULD WE DO WITHOUT THE LOVING GRANDMOTHERS OF THE WORLD?

I at least got to enjoy the loving adoration of my real true blood biological grandmother & always in my home as this grandmother came with the her last born son who married my mother. She is and always be the salvation of my soul and identity as I and she bonded like a true son and mother, this granny was the most magnificent person I had ever seen in our family, able to have power over the elements thru I now know is paranormal abilities, so to her I especially dedicate this the story of really, her grandson and son. Some normalcy returned for once after this heroin of a grandmother (buela) more than the rejection from the mother cat.

This Florence Nightingale mother's logic to toughen up a child not yet recovered from the shock of child imprisonment with extreme starvation & black hole pit for the cell kept in, no light was included, I was just in darkness defies reasoning. But, the torture and bruising would be now be heaped on by a much older brother who was ordered to do this on a regular basis, to see if this would make me forget the abuses committed to me by her, and she liked to point this out to this older brother, she had elevated him to her position of master torturer of this weakling runt of a kitten she was determined to starve to death and bruise-up the rest of runtifying technique that the Cat's learn at Cat mothering school. Were it not to this grandmother that showed me all of the different and myriad ways that a person can show love & I mean wholesomely as this was the only way that this mothering of mothers knew how to show love and she also turned out to be one of my most important symbolic mentors of my entire life.

HOW DID THIS NATIVE SON FIND OUT HE HAS TERETT'S SYNDROME? Well, let's see, it's not to hard to figure out that something is terribly wrong when you cannot hold an eating utensil steady as if you looked like you had Parkinson's disease, but you are only 12 so it couldn't be that. The food would fling all over the place & I would be with some piers eating in the cafeteria when this behavior would then make them laugh, but this mortified me as I already had noticed that I was experiencing this ill nervous control. When my siblings noticed this in me they found no reason to condemn and humiliate me but there wasn't much of any concern as to try to find some sort of remedy or diagnosis of this as this as you might expect cost money which I of course wasn't worth funding on. This condition was not uncommon at the time as it turns out, but not very much was know about this condition at the time, so many of the medical community still regarded as mysterious, perplexing, and not much information therefore had yet been compiled about this new mysterious malady! When I first showed up with it, my siblings were the ones that found that I might be in a public arena and say something like "wet pussy" 1st scary then horrifying & then they'd warn that I was going to be told on. Believe me, I became as horrified as they were and I'd complain to them that I didn't really think this to say it, it just came out I don't understand either & then I'd start to cry because I knew that I was now probably starting to display a new form of self injury that I had become so good at. This had to be my newest version 2.0 version of my self deprecation which I owed so genuinely to the abovementioned abuse mother. This became about the only way that I now regarded this mother. This mother that so loved torturing infants I know did have a heart and it did hurt her to see her SON manifesting these ticks in this awful way, but I also saw fear in her eyes but this fear seemed to be mingled with her fear for both herself as well as her fear for me. As if a child like myself may be able to know, this crazy mother would ask me things like, "What's wrong sonny, what seems to be troubling you, might there be something that I could do?" "My forever Florence Nightingale was now actually exhibiting concern for her beaten down little "hotito", this in and of itself frightened me, so I treated this new behavior of mine secretly & now would proceed down a path of isolating myself much the same way that this mother wanted me to be anyway, so what was going to be missed anyway. This had to come about as a result of my puberty shock which I experienced simultaneously, wow, people the life I've endured, it's a wonder that I can compile all of these memories most of which I had almost forced myself to forget. The sad truth though that even though somebody must have stolen my rough manuscript, and I only wanted to have to go thru remembering this once, now as I go thru having to do this—again, yet, I'll have to do this again. Sin embargo, I know that now I'll even remember more. Anyway, once I would go thru this behavior & treatment, feeling totally worthless & an embarrassment to myself and all my family, nothing would improve but the most that would be done to improve my development would be to enroll me in a boy scout program so I might learn better how to embrace the doctrine of that of being a boy at the tender age of 11. Did I say boy, yes, I did & I didn't say the doctrine of being a girl. In terms of the Tourettes syndrome that I exhibited, there would never be anything done about this I still live with this at this age of 58, but it is like 90% diminished & usually only if I inform someone, they won't catch on but even at this old of an age this bothers me & I have always been slightly vain, so folks, just how do you think this affects me.

THINK FOLKS, WHAT DO YOU^A NATIVE SON SHOULD DO SINCE TERETS SYNDROME CURIOUSLY HAS SUDDENLY DEVELOPED & AS A RESULT OF WHAT

I'll tell you the what was, probably the reason that this horrible affliction came about that I didn't have yet before the strike starvation to the skull and the subsequent what I survived in what I lovingly refer to as my pit.

Today I recorded a piece about a boy that had this Tourettes, so this made me feel somewhat good about myself, even though I am writing this terrible novel that this illness has affected my entire life. Any lover I have ever had I have totally repelled by my Tourettes syndrome behavior in some way or another because you see, I also have the other injuries that makes be a bit like a nagging wife or just a constant complainer! Even my wife told me that thinking about this stuff all the time could lead to my ruination. It wasn't that I was thinking about this all the time, but the memories were so domineering and constantly recurring even when I would try to forget all of my terrible memories, they started to become repetitive flashbacks, & was this a result of compulsive behavior that this hate mother was wanting to design. If so, people, she was now better than she knew she was. Now, did you know that people like me who are brown count far less if they have such an illness, lord these sort definitely should be put away, was the feeling that I was left with, & remember this mother was not below using the I'm white race card on her own son, surprise, & this Spanish complected mother (lily white) did just that. I never did say that this mother had won the best mother of the year award now, did I? "The tease of having been registered to become a boy scout for one mere year is pitiful to me now as this anemic effort of hers did little to amend the ills of the past which had been brought on only by her very own hands. I'll try to conclude this on an uplifting note, the boy that I video graphed today that has Tourettes was about 10 & has published his new book that is about his struggles & the TV channel lists another channel that I can lookup and find out more about this dreaded illness and I plan to do just that tonight. I'm all over these my ills of the past that I'm just writing about, so people, root for me & just maybe this boy can lead me to how I might be an adult version of what might could happen in the wrong way when such illnesses are left undiagnosed and unattended. Imagine my comparing myself to a ten year old when I possess approximately the equivalent to a Bachelors degree, 51 cr. hrs. at a University, a H.S. Diploma, A Certification in Word Processing and I'm also a Certified commercial Art, and lastly, I took two computer literacy courses, yet I lack confidence that I might be able to accomplish this book, and it isn't because I feel I lack skills, but it's because I have these terrible self Proclaiming Raiders who are claiming responsibility for having caused my book to suddenly disappear, the rough draft that is. I just know that this preliminary submissible copy that I'm writing from impromptu because that happened can't leave my sight & I sleep with it under my bed, pretty bad folks, when things get to that point isn't it? I have also seen featured episodes of people who have had Tourettes & they have literally caused Govts. to stand down, I can understand why, yet, this Govt. entrapped this Tourettes victim, and went one further and denied him his constitutional right of being marandized, & they didn't think that I was smart enough to know that I was being violated! That was their worse mistake, to underestimate me a former Regional Secretary for the organization that we Mexican American's at the time had called The Raza Unida in Ohio, and I was thoroughly offended by this having been done to such a native son of the United States of America, I guess this made me feel that because I was dark complected & being arrested basically because I was gay & being suspected of lewd behavior, this meant that I was going to have my name smeared so this puny little hick town known for being the Klan capital of our nation is now going to sock it to this gay Chicano, what a though, unqualified success for them. Even it was one of their rookies that didn't yet know what he was doing who did this to me, still laws of our Govt. were broken & I was the one that was made to pay money to a Parole Officer for 6 months based on what I call a bogus arrest by an inexperienced rookie a violation in the worse way and yes, I had taken law and gotten a B on the final exam so I did know that my constitutional rights had been violated. I also know that there's not two separate set of laws that one set is applied to white suspected law violators & another entirely different set of laws that should specifically be applied to minorities & or gay suspects, & guess what, I was in the fortunate position of belonging to 2 maybe 3 strikes against me classes; gay, Mexican American, and appearing somewhat darker complected as I constantly had to be working in the sun. This was profiling at its best if I ever saw anything like that, this was it's ugly face. Violating me America, after the way that this horror mother has gotten away with, this tiny town finds it so easy to look past me as I do not appear to be a threat. This town doesn't how I know how I could get this entire state in trouble for having denied a local business owner with business licenses & a trailer park owner, I should have contacted the justice Department right then, but, I knew better than that in this tiny town's mindset towards minorities & gays.

I also know for a fact that the way that I was approached & spoken to by this vice rookie constituted violating the laws of entrapment as the officer denied being a vice cop after I had asked him several times, at least 4 that I clearly remember! That, my friends is entrapment when after several lies were mouthed by the rookie, anything that may or may not have happened this would have been a mute point. [In] conclusion so that I can shift my gears to the topic that should be the most germane topic that this entire story is about, these violations that were committed to an adult business owner/operator the system got to get away with much the same way that this torture mother did & they were allowed to obtain large sums of money from a very small struggling business, humiliate a professional who was literally running an entire neighborhood, and I was also subjected to freezing temperatures which ever since I had been entombed by this mother would easily cause me to go into hyper thermal convulsions like when they 1st. removed/retrieved me from my hole my mom had made for our punishment. I did experience hyper thermal event in that cell they put me in, but I asked for a blanket & at least they gave me a thin sheet that did little to help, yet, thanks to this small request which took a long to get to me, I didn't have a heart attack or anything like that, and this kind of thing can happen. Although this happened a long time ago, it plays a big role in the demise of an American son that much like this torture mother leads and contributes to my Thelma and Louise type of mindset that this system along with parenting, are totally out to ruin and get a hard working bloke just like those two girls were.

This story people like it or not is a story of all that can go wrong in a person's life that has this illness that is much a mystery to the medical community at the time of the understanding of this malady. I did crack up as a combined result of managing a thoroughly racist neighborhood along with having this condition & although I knew that something was wrong with me, nobody wanted to acknowledge that I had this wrong with me much less do anything to help me deal with it. You would think that the lover I had might be concerned about this, but he didn't seem to care in the least and instead he seemed to be using this weakness of mine as his opportunity to pipe into my ears that even though I had certain defects, nothing would take away from the beauty that I still had. He would also seem to perceive as my weakness to the extent that he felt that he could get away with his painful sex and his horrible talk about pedophilia with me & including my very own son and I strongly emphasize to any readers, none of this kind of talk or even referring to in such a light was acceptable to me much less I did I even want to consider acting out on such a horrible idea! This boy that I at his age of 18 months seemed to think that he could drive, so with his cute mother looking on & holding our only little daughter I'd place little Julian between my legs and told him I'd control the pedals until his legs grew long enough, he actually steered and would remember to put the blinkers on! Why would I possibly think about pedophilia with my beautiful child when I already had had all this? I know that one could be both a homo and a pedo too I guess, but I never have been interested in children this way & I never will be so inclined.

I INHERIT THE PIT THAT I'M KEPT IN FOR WHAT FELT LIKE AN ETERNITY

Yes people, I said I inherited this pit that I was kept in, and it's true as creepy as this may seem, this old brick school with its mini little child dungeon that is beneath the bathroom floor is listed in my father's holdings that he leaves to us 6 remaining children. I already walked thru this old school house with a sister, but I didn't lift up the trap door to this crawl space, I just wanted to get out of this bldg. as soon as I could. It was icy cold that day but it still had the potential to bring back a cascade of horrible memories as the entire bldg. seemed to me like a dungeon, yet once, in the above living part, I remember having at least a few good memories yet now as I reflect back, they are definitely few and far between. I suspected that this sister had this inclination of denying any negative events or memories she never has any memory of but her expression deceives her. Still, I feel compelled to allow this sister to have her right to forgetting the way I did until things mounted to the point that they did when I would let it get to me. I even remember once when I and my then common law wife out of poverty were forced to live in it in the 70's and in my sleep, I felt a super heavy hoof on my chest & it was bearing down so heavily that I could barely breathe, & I smell could the stench of something like a goat, is this house possessed?

I also could feel his warm breath over me but I was so paralyzed with fear that I knew that the only way to deal with this was to not open my eyes, not respond, and I knew that I couldn't wake up my wife. Needless to say, this worked & to this day, I feel that there must be truth to afterworld beings, paranormal activities, but I don't necessarily want to compare this to ghosts. In the past when considering all of the injuries that I sustained in this school house in the crawl space, I never considered that this house could have been the object of a paranormal presence in it, but then who or what could have caused a mother of all things to treat a child a way that I was treated in that govt. bldg.? Was there a torturer that had been a teacher that had taught or even lived in that bldg., even to muse over such ideas does me no good whatsoever. So you see people, I have even exhausted the ideas that may have been the causes to lead this crazy mother down the torture child avenue. The truth of the matter is that my mother was so tortured when she was an infant that her injuries got to her so she in turn also wanted to inflict pain and psychological manipulations the same way that I was told that her father had inflicted to every one of the children that he and my grandma had. Mom also liked to recount the anecdote, when this grandfather had their frequent fights she was made as a tiny infant to watch as this torturer of humans had his way right in the presence of this tiny little child along with 1 or two others. She told us that this was a regular event and the pig liked to drag his wife by the mane or the hair of the head, then he would brag to anybody in the house who was listening and emphasize that anybody in the house that didn't do his bidding to the letter was subject to getting this kind of treatment also. In the family setting of this mother's of mine, there was a total of 5 children who most of them grew up with this kind of ignorant child abuse by a drunken tyrant, is it any wonder that this mother would later in life find it so easy to torture her own children herself. This bigger than life grandparent had much on his shoulders, raising children during the great depression, however, being a big band musician & also a coal miner shouldn't excuse him from everything from child incestuous rape to the treatment aforementioned of the grandmother, but for these poor children and wife, would be all they would ever know, until the divorce in the 50's long after my mother had left the child rearing setting. Some of these children who I later grew to know quite well would recount of how their dad had actually met such illustrious famous people as many of the big band era band leaders among some of them; Benny Goodman, Louis Armstrong, Xaviar Cougat, Tommy Dorsey, and Duke Ellington and a couple of others as this grandfather had become quite well known himself so these already famous artists were happy to meet him.

Was my childhood abuse & torture indirectly connected to this musician who was also a womanizer, child torturer, wife beater, coal miner, & somewhat absentee parent as he had to travel high and low to both coal mine & do gigs throughout the U.S. of A. I don't think that I have any doubt about that matter as he even managed to inflict an indirect injury to me, yes, I did say me people as I suffered lime burns throughout all of my hands one time when he was training and assisting me in the construction of a foundation that he and I built for my mother's temporary living arrangement which was a brand new doublewide mobile home. This torture grandparent warned me not to place my hands directly in the mortar & I of course didn't know better, but I did this anyway, only to have to hear him laughing uncontrollably when I ended up with holes all over my hands because I actually didn't believe this grandfather who had known all these people. I guess I also had this bigger than life vision of what this grandfather was, boy did I ever get a rude awakening. The time that this grampa and I built this foundation, he was already in his middle 80's yr. of age & I just didn't think that this parent figure would be capable of not caring enough to being this callous with his grandson. All he had to do was say, if you don't listen, you'll eventually end up with tiny holes all over your hands. Even though it did not hurt at the time that I touched handled this mortar, after about 6 Hr. it will eat thru your skin. Live and learn, die and forget it all. From having been steered the wrong way by these mental relatives way too often I had lost all trust in any of them including this evil grandparent, therefore I would end up sustaining injuries even by my mother's dad and at a time when I'm making great sacrifice as I was not getting paid to build this very expensive foundation for my mother and dad. They knew they would have had to pay thousands had I not stepped up to the plate along with this super abusive grandpa, & his old over inflated and exagerated ego. All my life whenever I'd ask about this grandfather, her dad, I'd get, "you really don't want to know him, you are going to be disappointed," and boy was she ever right, but as I said, I now have little trust in any of these blood relatives of mine.

One thing is for sure, I now truly believed all of the horrible tales that this mother had recounted about the abuses of this father of hers who now reveled in that he now had been able to cause an injury to one more of his decedents. Such is the family that this native son of yours America came from, and so wire the frugal & struggling parents of my distant past.

Now I ask my readers, do you think that there might have been a legacy of abuse that contributed to this mothers proclivity and propensity to injuring her very own children? Yes, I'd certainly believe her so, the mother who according, to her suffered the worse abuse incl. torture & rape, would raise 6 children. This most tortured child of her broody I would end up being the worse abused that I have ever seen, her very own torture child, the way she must have seen her own father have. From these abuses would come Tourettes Syndrome type mannerisms, and OCD & severe distrust of anybody to the point of becoming rabid. When I was saved and discovered that is taken out of that pit, I stayed in shock for many years, but I was still taunted and neglected to the point of abnauseum. My Tourettes has come back particularly bad due to the fact of having to remember all this since my rough draft I believe was stolen but not displaced. I know how to work it though so that I can make it almost virtually go away. I've developed excellent control over this malady over the years.

Somehow this law breaking mother truly wanted to convince her son that she truly was responsible for my genital injuries that I mentioned earlier,—but she wanted me to remember that this was an outcome of her contempt for me. So, you see, I couldn't win with her, which was what she thought, but at the time that I was trying to enjoy a sort of wedded bliss with miraculously my childhood sweetheart is when she wants to stress that, she told me that she had decided to ruin this kitten who didn't do any good for her litter.

Now you must know by now if you've been keeping up with the theme of this mother's propensity to inflict psychological abuse, "you worthless hotito", you puny weakling, "you nigger, I hate the very sight of you," "Why didn't you die all those times when you were so close, why did you live and the other 3 beautiful ones die, I hate you, "te odio", she'd say not so lovingly. Yes, the torture mother and deprivation master, was at it again & now after I have even officially left the nest, but she just couldn't get it. Now I've been messed with once more by her and this time she has involved the one that I was planning to have children with.

Now her sweet little son who was pulled out of the HOLE, the same one that this nearly killed and still suffers the Tourettes humiliation to this day, now her son was going raise the bar to the bitch of a mother that had been his misfortune to have been doled out, the torture mother of torture mother's. Now, I'm going to teach the psychological torturer a lifelong psychological torture for her to forever remember when I had to run down the street in broad daylight naked when I was 3yrs. old, much too old & old enough to know better, but again as it was now, this was a knee jerk reaction to the chakra injury of my male chakra area & howl ended up responding. Eat that and weep. Would you want all these tortures? This injury that this evilest of mothers so aggressively wanted to take claim will be directly connected by someone that is already a Tourettes victim like when I went thru the shock of puberty be galvanized and forever psychologically connected to and with this mother's proclaimed hatred. This hatred, the hatred that has always been alive & probably even grew more intense as time progressed is forever burned in my brain & connected with flashing her.

Are you beginning to get the gist of what the main premise of this book is, yet? That when a disorder is not diagnosed much less acknowledged less treated, that what mistakenly might be diagnosed as only minor problems and dismissed as nervous disorder's, how treating a real true disorder in this way could deteriorate to this most horrible and Life devastating tragic, worse case scenarios. I have no doubt that I did not have my physical nervous ticks, & such things as stuttering before I was subjected to all of the mistreatments by demented adults that should have been nurturing me. I made a promise to my mother that because she had tried to ruin my sexual apparatus as a punishment that I regarded as overstepping her bounds too late anyway. I know that her having done the punishment she regarded as necessary to curb my sexual appetite was without a doubt criminal on her behalf. Isn't that when people who commit such offenses are supposed to be prosecuted? Not in this case, in fact this mother actually told me that she was under a Judge's orders, that she had been told that she had to intervene in order for me not being arrested, & to this I say BUNK, as I spent almost all of my time with this mother as her travelling interpreter, so I never had seen any cops, nor any letters from any Judges.

This was another of this mother's lie's to try to discourage any blame or any fault for her having been caught by me accusing her of having broken the law yet again by abusing me even at this ripe old age, how dehumanizing and denigrating & humiliating. Still, I knew this went along with, "They always want to blame it on the mother, & they never think about all that a mother has to go thru to bring these children to the world & make them all be upright citizens," and the litany went on abnauseum. The "(WORD) f'd with my genitals again, and I also knew what it meant to be circumcised as I had also gone thru this at the age of 4 & don't ask me why I developed this drip like condition that I now remember seemed to be something like syphilis? Now, don't forget I had been sold to this uncle for the upstairs quarter he had to pay the rent, & remember, I would be included, how horrific to think that I might have had syphilis at this young of an age & then had to endure a circumcision to cover this up!

Anyway, I had already been down the working in the Japetto's workshop area ordeal, & now at this age of 20, I didn't want this B' of a mother reveling in front of me and even to her torture friends about this, but this she would go on to do. If I had contracted something like gonorrhea from this uncle, now as so many other was the one that was going to be made to suffer as the outcome of someone else's blunders.

Sometimes to me it just seemed like this mother knew how to push things to the edge with these rigid old fashioned views, her hatred for the male species, her depraved regard for the suffering of human life totally like some kind of sociopath, that is a person who can act out unconscionably, the cold heart that this mother displayed to me was that cold look that the shark eyes cat has when mother cat goes to snuff out one of her unwanted and excessive baggage extra mouth to feed and clean up after and many other things to worry about providing for look. My mother cat had this look in her eyes often!

AND NOW ABOUT HER FALSELY CLAIMED PSYCHIC ABILITIES &
POSSIBLY MY UNPROCLAIMED REAL TRUE ONES

By the time that I've reached the ripe old age of 10, I seem to have a sense of peace as a couple of years of prosperity are enjoyed by all. At the time, I know that I have had to suppress volumes of sadistically inflicted injured memories but up to that age, I've now been having mother dearest's brand new version of abuse, and this was primarily of the psychological variety. After remember the forever taunts about being sissified & I must include that all of the siblings were rooted on & encouraged to perform her latest version of these psychological taunts after she had told me that she was going to try to change me into a girl when I was about 2 yrs. old, now these taunts is what I had to be subjected to. These would be how I would be treated for most of my life save that of a brief period when mother briefly experienced a revelation, & when I had been urging for her to enroll me in the local boy scout program, she enrolled me to one mere year, then I was told icily by her as I probably enjoyed myself too much & was also experiencing a sense of emotional balance, there's no money for frivolous & stupid things like that for someone like you!

Why this mother had claimed to have abilities such as clairvoyance is beyond me, as the one who took over her job of being the mother to me did have psychic abilities, & I personally witnessed this grandmother go into a trance & perform what is known as environmental or elemental psychic abilities. My grandmother walked out to the porch when she had been told that the horizon was black as night which the fear was that a tornado or hurricane was eminent.

Grandma's forehead started to develop beads of sweat as she chanted her prayer and moved her hands to & fro as she put herself into definitely a kind of trance, and I had seen her put herself in this state before, now in her hand, she was wielding a machete, when like some kind of whoosh sound was heard, and it was this beautifully psychic grandmother striking the machete thru the air in the direction of the Night type horizon & it was the afternoon part of the day when this happened. I instantly saw the two sides to the black horizon start to form as my grandma watched on with satisfaction and a sense of relief also was evident. I knew or had heard that she had this before, but this time I wanted to see it with my own eyes, as the other times I only had heard her doing this but I hadn't be there, so this time I had to see it to believe it, but no part of this grandmother displayed any kind of smugness about such abilities the way the conceited braggart mother had, & by the way, to me this means that the mother had cried wolf, so I now believed that the mother was the hoax & I now came to know that the real psychic one of the family was fortunately for me the sweet granny who would mentor and raise me! So that explained the oo's and ah's that I had heard my siblings exclaim whenever the grandmother to all of this would have to do this to protect her still considered family, how lucky was I to later get to have this bigger than life matriarch for my new mother & with possibilities of being mentored in psychic skills to boot, wow!

At the age of 19 when I experienced the nervous breakdown that shocked the entire clan & family, I went into my withdrawn and meditation mode & commenced to read myself out of this clinical depression, as I knew that there would be no medical or psychological help coming, correct? I was from a background of abject poverty and I knew it, so I braced myself for whatever else might happen. What happened was I cried for over a year for my identity *&* for fact that I didn't have one now I ask you if that is physically possible, well, the mother seemed to have lobotomized my identity on more than one occasions, now what was this deceitful *&* maniacal absent emotionally all my life up to, do you think at this breakdown point she's able to still inflict emotional abuse with starvation included? You bet your bippy she could, I was after all a adult that wasn't being productive & I definitely wasn't paying for the food I was eating, now was I? The biological mother kept her eyes on the Fridge & I don't put it her past her to put such things as her woman medicines like estrogen pills broken up so that I might be more suitable for what she might be cooking up, & I just watched this grandma and she would always be there to protect me from this torturous mother, wow, what a hell of an untenable situation. This beautiful grandmother would reinforce me by saying such things as I love you my precious sonny, don't let anything she (cat mother) would say, upset & emphasize that I could no wrong to her she'd beg me to get better as seeing me like this also was taking its toll on her & she'd tell me that she was lighting her candles & with prayer's in my behalf so soon things would turn up for the better for me. And so I struggled to hang on to some kind of sanity, until the day would come when I would have enough courage to just make it out that dreaded front door of our house, but I sure hoped that nobody would see If I ever did get the courage that is.

I now have developed severe agoraphobia which I had also lived with only this condition came on gradually, but this disorder had never caused me to stay inside of a house for this amt. of time when I feared leaving the house for more than 18 months. During this protracted time that my nervous breakdown lasts, I in retrospect regard the time imprisoned in this horrible house a time that goes along with the time lost in the pit below the school house, that terrible torment time of mine and my mothers. This would also be a time when I would develop certain psychic abilities also from the kind of literature that I was reading. Do you remember reading about this grandmother's abilities, well, my abilities go back further than you might think. Eventually I ask this psychic grandmother if she might be able to be teach how to also perform such miracles as the cloud parting, & her eyes were suddenly widened so wide that I knew that unwittingly I have to have struck a nerve and as I read later when I was in the meditative mode (studying, praying, meditating (TM), that she was living up to the description of a spiritual leader in not addressing my query's and staying in this state of humility and grace that this elder always manifested to me & I dedicate this book to her the grandson that may have inherited these abilities from not the real mom, but from the grand mom. Also, included in the studies that I was independently studying was the ancient ability of soul travel, but although one can admit to delving into this, one can not disclose any of the experiences that one might have been fortunate enough to have accomplished. I, like my grandma had to learn to keep these things in, or risk loosing any gains that might have been made, and so such literature is written & by organized religions that have been around far longer that the Christian religions have been, by a couple of thousand years in some cases depending on the religion one is talking about. I embarked down a path none of my family has ever taken, that of the desire to leave the physical body that I lived in as the one that I lived in was too intolerable, but, you know this should not be a reason to want to experience any out of body experiences, yet for pathetic me, as I just wanted to leave this world of torture I mostly had known, were it not for this adoring and mentor of a grandmother, I would surely would have been sunk. My cute grandmother was like a Spanish version of the Beverly Hillbillies, only with a Mid Wife slant. Granny in the Hillbillies also had her brews, remember? Anyway, she had her size & looks & if you picture one, you can see the other, My granny wasn't dressed unless she finally had placed one of her 50 or so many handmade aprons, and she was also as pure as the driven snow, and devoutly Catholic, and she claimed that any powers which might be as of a spiritual nature, she claimed came from her sweet Jesus, as he was the man in her life.

During my earliest school experiences when I was in kindergarten is when I 1st. remember experiencing what must have been my real true 1st paranormal abilities which I would have smacked out of me by my piers as I would be accused of having the devil in me simply because I was able to start fires when I was not yet, 5, but just a few days later around June 1st. school starts, & I was born the 7th. of June. I started school at the age of 4, now that tells you they want to get rid of one more child to take care of, at least that what I heard my mother tell some of her hateful torture club girlfriends.

My mom also told me that if I displayed these abilities to the children at school, that surely they would tell me that I had the devil in me, so I of course as I did not trust this which of a mother who fee Is it necessary to enroll a child that has known nothing but abuse to kindergarten at 4, well, was I going to have to listen or be inclined to that. As far as I can tell, the guilt ended up getting to me along with knowing better than to think that showing that I had this ability didn't garner me any friends, & I remember two girls going to the classroom crying & pointing at me because they thought I was or had the devil in me, when this now after all this time in today's times that we live in was nothing more than my possessing paranormal abilities, and I still be-that I possess these traits, & I'm now trying to be able to harness these skills, to see how they might be able to be helpful/useful to me or the world in the future. I'm proud to say that this grandmother was descended from people in Spain, I just don't know how long ago our people came over, but her mom was blue eyed, & a cousin from her side of the family who lived nearby also had two children that were blond and blue eyed, so yes, our Mexican heritage does have roots in Spain too. The Spanish were don't forget once responsible for a Holy War to convert the entire world spiritually to Catholicism, but I wouldn't necessarily attribute any of this granny's gifts solely to this Christian spiritualism.

MY PSYCHIC ABILITY DEMONSTRATED BY ME NOW DID SO AT AGE 16

I have to digress, as now I also have to shed a negative light on paranormal abilities with evil intent underlying, but manifested 35 Mi. away as in a rage, with my head hung down & beads of sweat forming on my forehead, the same cousin that was responsible for my near death beating up by a 15 yr. old brother, I was kicked about like a limp sack of potatoes, I had sustained the worse beating up of my life by this muscle bound brother who was already earning money bailing hay. By now at approximately the age of 15, I'm having sad flashbacks of this event, along with flashbacks of other insidious ways that this cousin & my brother had attempted to mock & humiliate me & I was a relative of both of them, when I jumped out of my skin as the phone rang, & my sister uttered the words so sorrily, that the cousin mentioned who caused my own brother to nearly kill me was now in the hospital & in a coma, out of which he would stay in for about 1 yr. It was exactly what I was focusing on because they felt as if they wished that I were dead, now he would come out of his f'n coma with only the wheelchair as a friend, and this brother who was so close of a so called friend of his would never look him up, so I ask, you as a reading public, was this utter coincidence, or did these blood relatives push a cousin with potentially paranormal abilities too far? Now that brother had already gone to war in Nam, but I surely didn't want to aim any ill events to be coming his way & I only was missing him in my life but I just felt further abandoned by when I wanted this brother to become one of my strongest lifelines. I considered him a hero in my life though, for he was fighting an unpopular war yet people forget that any American soldier who is fighting a war for us, is ultimately fighting to preserve freedom for all the people of the world which also includes protecting our freedoms. God bless you good brother I long since forgave you for your sins, & I pray you forgave me for mine, & no hard feelings, we were all made to do her bidding. But this book is only about me and the injuries I survived & sometimes, I'm amazed that I also lived to write about it.

This mean spirited cousin who would make fun of me and who would end up in a wheel chair and end up permanently bavoso, (drooling) who I always showed symptoms of psychotic behavior before he had that terrible accident the same time that I was wishing so intensely for him to be horribly hurt as an ultimate payback, this same cousin, who never knew that I had wished for this, would later tell me that "I wasn't such a bad cousin for a Gay Blade, so my poor cousin even though at the time he got hurt was the class president, performing live performances as a child prodigy lead base guitar player at 11, he still displayed psychosis & over preoccupation with his sexuality for not yet being in puberty, and I think that also spells something rotten in Denmark for acting in such a way before becoming a quadriplegic that he preferred to dummy down to partial pelagic, but he does drool, and fall over all the time & causes my poor aunt to have to haul him around all over the place, that is if she is still even living along with if he is, if so, hello from the gay blade. But, this story isn't about this aunt and her red headed step child type son, that mocked his sissified cousin, so on with the germane, but this was the fabric of my life. Needless to say, and in spite of the obnoxiousness of this cousin with the meanness to mock me, I forever after he had the accident of being hit on a bicycle by a car, felt guilt though I knew that to admit this could mean mortal injury to me by the torture mother as you know this was the son of her sister. This must have been what did tick off my mother when one time when I was complaining about all of my mistreatment, I blurted out to her and again with contempt the way she liked to rub in salt into a wound too! Maybe that's why I got the terrible pay back from her that I did.

I told that (word) that I hung down my head and focused all the energy to my brain and what I was concentrating about so that it might come to happen, and so that was how I had managed to do that, & I had done this mistakenly & I had wished that I never had, but I wanted to find out if I was still capable of outdoing any of my other rivals, like I had when I had started fires & I was never able to get this ability back. I argued with my eyes tearing up that due to their mistreatment, now look what he was going to have to learn to live with. Of course, she made me stop talking about it & asked me to promise to never admit this to her or speak of it again, just like I was asked when I had started the fires.

I wanted to believe that it was coincidence, but that is too accurate of an event when one is wishing for such a thing to be so. Now my ticks seemed to increase as a result of a feeling of guilt with regards to that sad event that really did occur in all of our lives.

Later this small family of 5 would break up and become 4 & come to live by us & became an integral part of my life. This was the saddest thing I had ever seen, with my illiterate stepping up to the plate & building a 49 ft. ramp to assist my cousin up to their back door of their mobile home which my mother had financed for her sister. One thing that I want to emphasize, is that we Latin's are tight, and we always strive to live up to the extended family & nuclear family blueprint. Now this would fill my empty life with the tender cousins that I adored who came to live right at our adjacent lot that these two sisters would develop together. Just think, I had to keep this in all the time that I lived by them when they came to live by us.

PSYCHIC ABILITIES CONTINUED

Going back to my agoraphobic dungeon that my mother largely contributed to comprising the major part by way of all of the above inflicted injuries to body and soul, and the time that I was going thru the breakdown, & I didn't really know what this was that I was going thru, but I was truly trying to figure out who I was & why I wasn't able to face the world anymore. I just had this intuition that if I delved by reading into the thoughts and beliefs of other religions, that I might come to the point that I might like myself again, because, as you know, that you can't learn to love, until you learn to love yourself. Anyway, as I dove into the beliefs of other thought systems, and ways of viewing things like my homosexuality for instance, I did eventually come to accept who I had came to be, and I also believe that this is another time that I almost died in a dungeon, and I can still see my mom's wide eyes whenever she'd rarely look in on me, as a look of is the egg yet hatched, or is the chick not yet ready to hatch or did it hatch yet, some kind of quirky look that only that mysterious crazy parent could concoct.

I read up on soul travel thru an ancient discipline of bi-location & the name of the book that I studied is ECKENKAR, after thoroughly reading the book with the aid of entities that one is to pray to, but with the self absolutely removed so as to be able to become disconnected with this world and all of its physicality's, & such things as greed, lust, and avarice governing our minds, only then can one experience what it might mean to be in another kind of type of experience such as a realm where also our existence is on a different molecular or ethereal type of body so that one could possibly much more easily be able to use this body for astral projection. Now you all must be saying that, "sure you did, and I can human transport too," I actually according to the discipline am not ever even supposed to ever admit to this or speak about the deities who one prayed to, but, trust me, it wasn't devil worship, and I did get answers for things that I genuinely and sincerely had prayed for, so I give thanks to these guides also, & I also believe that I will always be under their watchful eyes, as I have never forgotten how these powers had carried me thru when I had been at my most dismal lowest bottom of the lowest part & time of my clinical depression.

I'm not talking about such things and in such ways to be in any way braggadocios, and I only have gone thru life & been constantly suppressed about these gifts I may have had. I also may have developed some of late, as I have seen ball lightening, and more than once, and for the past 15 yrs. anywhere I live, the immediate closest transformer's, those that provide electric to our houses, always end up having to be moved because they will invariably blow. If they don't just blow, they get hit by lightning, and no other transformers in the area do this but where I live, and usually when this happens, I'm usually having one of my rages of anger, which I really believe is what affects this outcome.

The neighbors to the back who had crossed me one too many times had a series of spontaneous combustion at a time when I had gotten enraged with these people for one reason or another, & did this combined with my electrical power over transformers blend with ball lightening, or was it my old fire starter abilities showing up again?

It isn't that I didn't believe in the Christian religious doctrines, as you heard, this grandmother and possibly psychic mentor derived her spiritual power's she professed from the devoutness to the Roman Catholicism that she solely believed in & she didn't know about the things that I was spiritually studying about. I knew that she never would been able to understand these studies & she might have protested anyway. However, the Christian Catholicism it had seemed to me had been the reasons that I had gone under the injurious control of this morbid & depraved parent, that professed that her religion and her god was guiding her hands with regards to my punishment, & her ways of using guilt to try to control.

I never turned to atheism, even though the Catholic version of Christianity had, I have no doubt been the main reasons that I sustained all of my injuries from the gash to the head to the rope marks on my back from the time that I had been tied up & I knew that these parents were going to think that a tyke as small as 8 or 10 months might forget, but I remember almost every single torture that I received from these parents. I have what looks like stretch marks at the small of my back, & I sustained these rope burns because I was what they thought low enough & small enough to abuse this way, so they roped me like a dog & I do have these scars where I said I do.

When abuses get to adults, things can get out of hand when like just when pressure builds up too high in a soda bottle, & you take off the cap then suddenly, the foam is gushing up like a geyser, so can abuses of the past that are pent up or suppressed inside come to a head like this too.

I can't make any apologies to anyone for this or the outcome of getting to such a state of despair, but what I can suggest is if a person shows signs of emotional despair the way I had at so many times in my life, better guide such a person to not a religious counselor, but to a good Psychiatrist, or at least a confident social worker to guide me the rest of the way. For that kind of a solution, I know, you would have to come from money. And by now if you've read this far, you already know that their was a bond between my mom and my dad, that no money would ever be expended on this sibling, and their bond would ring true whenever I break down would again as so many times before, so I would have to ultimately end up having to turn to something, now wouldn't I? I had always been fascinated by such things as TM, meditation, hypnosis, etc. so what better sense did it make but to turn when such things as organized religion has failed you, by way of this mother's abuses & claiming that this belief, system warranted such punishments.

I do remember seeing depictions of such tortures having been committed by the so called Holy Inquisition carried out by the Spaniards, so why was I having to endure these same tortures some 400 yrs. later, & why would this inure me to this kind of faith?

The hardest thing about this story to comprehend if you can, should the premise of the story, and you all should know that this premise is that a child who was beat to submission or die was also beat to point of developing OCD, TERETT'S syndrome, but instead of making things right for this poor soul, more condemnation with scorn & thorough hatred because the mother loved to fancy as having these superchildren, which I did not demonstrate but instead exhibited these Tourettes syndrome ticks & OCD, which only served to exacerbate & amplify these conditions that I was starting to exhibit to the world, & sometimes I especially tried to injury myself, but, in such a pathetic way to then be able to ask the mother if this self injury pleased her, as now I was saving her the trouble. Such ticks, and self injury mannerisms I did develop. Counting abnauseum or putting things all lined up in a row obsessively was one of my most dreaded mannerisms of hers and mine too as these seemed to be compulsive behaviors.

WHEN A HORRIBLE SET OF DEFECTIVE MANERISMS DEVELOPES RESULTING FROM SEVERE INFANT ABUSE WITH PSYCH TORTURE, NO INTERVENTION WILL BE SUCESSFUL

What intervention, who gives a F' about this insufferable puny child that is nothing but a nuisance, an embarrassment, & probably a living breathing form of evidence so my mother often displayed signs of actually having a conscience so, sometimes she would almost cry, ha ha. I don't think this cruelty deserves depicted this way, to me, she'd never be worth being regarded in as good a light like this. Sometimes the loony mother who I had to endure, liked to have long talks with me about my defects because maybe she wanted. me not to give her away as the torture mother that she was, so her conversations centered around on how I might be able to stop these uncontrollable spasms, ticks, or self-biting injuries, but I didn't want to have these creepy ways either, what a stupid mother I thought she was by now, & I knew she was mainly only thinking about her own reputation, that of not being found out of being a child torturer. That's exactly why nothing was ever done about my conditions, accept poking fun at me, mocking it, or laughing at it, what a son-of a bitch world this was turning into for me. "Oh, how heart breaking, "my mother might have said, but I was now quite used to her humiliation tactics of belittling things that should be regarded seriously. In other words she liked to shame me if I showed too many feelings as I seemed demonstrative to her this cold icy mom.

Besides representing being this insufferable son that was despised, with all of the above defects that she only exhibited embarrassment and shame over, don't forget, I was also her torture little hotito to forever kick around, & this is what her and her brood of children, no, make that followers of her superchildren of hers & of her making, which she showed that she was definitely proud of her carbon copies of her.

I am not going to go down in history as having been beaten down by this ignorant world, the Raiders (of the midnight variety), surely claiming victory over a land baron homosexual, who has all of the above defects, a torture mother who may be smugly grinning down in hell, where she certainly deserved to belong, yes grinning at all of my injuries that she saw fit to inflict simply because I was a little child that wasn't going to listen to an adult that was performing such brutal injuries, that she got away with not having to have served sufficient punishment by the State, but no, she's probably even laughing from her fire and brimstone home the way she & other Christian used to tell me that I was going to get. This is the way that the Redneck Raiders, or just Rednecks, who know that I was going thru so many issues that I didn't know if I was coming or going also found humor in such a breakdown, but I can't remember ever hearing anyone voicing any opinions about the horror's of the past that I have no doubt got me to be this way. No, now these so call Raiders, who were also neighbors directly living also a stone's throw from my ranch house the same way the poor murdered black girl had also lived.

THE VERY REASON THAT I'M NOT ASHAMED OF WRITING THIS GROTESQUE REAL TRUE ACCOUNT OF UNDIAGNOSED MANIFESTATIONS OF CHILD ABUSE IS:

This section I'll start out with the time that my mom decided to raise my voice a couple of octaves as you see I had a very froggy deep voice at about 3£ when she lead me to the kitchen because, her very own words, "I'm not going to have this little beast scare this whole entire household with his booming voice and at a whole of 3." I was going to endure the loss of this very boyish voice even though I hadn't even gone thru puberty yet, so even my big brother was for this, as he already was going thru this right of passage we all go thru. Mommy dearest made me drink some kind of fluid which burned immediately, caused me to choke and convulsively & involuntarily regurgitate, although this agent burned me severely, but after this treatment that she so viciously administered, the torture mother then laughed along with the siblings, her carbon copies, because when I went to speak, I now had a very high & shrill voice, when I at a 3 yr. old had this booming boisterous much louder even than this teenaged brother. This took about 3 to 4 weeks to recover from, & the only good memories that I retain from this terrifying event that really did occur to me is that when I regurgitated from the smell & potency of probably sulphuric acid that no doubt was what she used, is that I puked right straight in her direction right in her face, which I then saw her run to the sink as fast as she could, only to be too late, so my torture mother was now the victim of her own attempt at more child abuse. This torture mother now had something like acne pits in and on her face & it wasn't until much later that I'd put this together, that these were not acne scars, but a result of a time when, this child abuser yet again made that pathetic attempt to soften her son, & she thought that this would then not scare the world whenever I'd speak. I say that this was a good outcome now on my part, as this bitch of a mother now has gotten some of her own medicine, as her plan to raise my voice a couple of octaves did succeed, but her plan also backfired somewhat, as now she was going to have to go thru the rest of her life explaining and lying that her face was pitted due to acne scarring, but then, I knew better. I just described to the reader why I do not in the least feel ashamed about any of this book that I'm writing, get it yet? This attempt of hers to make me more like the rest of the girls and almost dwarf size son who loved nothing more than to give me this oversized son, as I was referred to, his good beating up, as he liked to put it, to show me who was the champion of this miserable brood. Most times, the mother was there rooting him on, and telling him that I was only getting what I deserved, and he was the good one, remember that I could refer to as a dwarf, hell, I got to hate this child beater brother himself a child, I even go as far as calling him midget, only in Spanish, which pronounced enanityo.

By now, I'm regarded as nothing but a rebel by these little robots of hers & by her. I caught hell all my life from this more for not wanting to be one of her goose stepping little monkey robots, but the way she stated very early on that she also in turn wanted to have one more girl with her attempts of raising my beautiful frog voice that I remember, my voice was way too deep & when I was picked on, I'd dominate with this adult male voice, & my siblings would cower down, & tell my mom that something had to be done about this dominant feature of mine.

On that, the other day I heard on television, that there's such a thing as a sibling effect, maybe my experiences of torture were the result of this effect, but I haven't see the news piece yet. In conclusion, this much older brother would beat the hell out of me until I would almost go unconscious & all the time the mom looking on with approval & the older brother looking back at her with love and affection, it was as if these two had a torture bond with regards to the extent to which he could pushed for torture me. This abuse mother looked fondly at her beater up son, as if he was a perfect image of her, sin embargo, her point in doing this was brutal humiliation & at the hands of more relatives. In conclusion, AND GOING BACK TO THE CHAPTER TITLE: why don't I feel any shame & no remorse about writing about such a torrid child abuse story encompassing all of the maladies of; Tourettes syndrome, OCD, Delayed Stress Syndrome (post traumatic), for three, and you might add to that, no one likes to go thru life with a whole set of symptoms t that came directly from child, adolescent abuse (psychological), and believe it or not, this abuse is even allowed to carry into adulthood, what do you think you would you have done? Well, I'll tell you what was done, "I flashed that f'n mother as my very 1st. victim & told her that if I didn't become a horrible abuser also the way that I was being brought up, that much more of this type of abuse & I did mention self abuse was to come. She must have been reading her tale about how a given mother had been able to control other children to the point of running an entire govt. I felt like a pawn in this mother's diabolical plan for me & when she said, "no son, please don't do that & talk to me in those terms, & why is it that you want to kill?" she'd ask coyly, so Naturally, I knew this mother was capable of having no feelings and was thoroughly capable of using reverse psychology, as she was much smarter than she let on, so I did not know whether this mother was using this ploy or not, as she always showed special attention not to pay me any attention, why would this be any different? I can hear my sister saying when regarding the way that my mother treated, "Mom played with Julian's head too much, yet, whenever I or my mother would win the other over, then she would always revert to her then again, I repeat, psychological torture type abuse, & eventually,—neither my mother nor would I give in to her passive aggressive new way that she now had mastered. Time now, was for more physical abuse. In my mother's eyes, to my horror, I saw a gleam in her eyes, as she contemplates how to go about her ultimate & probably her last one to that son, & she passive aggressed by no doubt slipping me the estrogen, which caused my foreskin to deteriorate on me until I had to have that circumcision. I can only surmise that this is the horrible way that she was planning & silently grooming me to have an operation in some way that she could injure my gonads, which later she would brag to me that this was the nice way that had been planned for me to subdue my male urges so that I could fit in with the rest of her brood. How horrible it is to think that this is a way that females in the Mex. society are matriarch's but the men are most apt to be womanizers, drunks, and they like their song & gambling too. Too bad that I am forced to shed ill light on our Chicano culture, but don't have OCD, Tourettes syndrome, &post traumatic stress syndrome and still be of the poor Chicano culture, cause there's some pretty poor remedies out there.

I knew that to complain in such a family & in such a poverty setting that these ills that beset me needed attention. If I did, it would only fall on deaf ears. Besides, I knew that it definitely made me feel like I was crying for too much from such poor parents, I actually felt sorry for them. One of my mother's favorite things to say regarding my complaints was to say that all I ever did was to complain, puras kejas, (nothing but complaints). This shrewd mother actually was trying to make me feel responsible for these injuries, that if I had listened, then I might not have sustained such injuries, she would taunt. still, I was also the one who figured out that my little brothers and sisters had better not get dressed in their Sunday best to go to their drowning because her husband was scarcer than hen's teeth. Why were children made to have to suffer this discord of our parents? I actually should have not cared a bit just like they hadn't cared a bit when I was in the pit, and I was made to try to gnaw on these already thoroughly gnawed bones. I should have not said a thing so that her other plot could have gone into place. Then, all of my bro's and sisters would have been forgotten bones at the bottom of the local reservoir! At times & behind these kid's backs, this mother expressed that I was more desirable as a child as my proportions were more normal, and I was finally a boy, & she'd say if just I just didn't have all the rest of those little rats.

This mother was a piece of work alright, going from one plot or diabolical escape plan from something she knew that she was now trapped in, or so she would express, especially if we were unruly. Even though these kids were also mean to me, I didn't want them dead.

So you see in one of her best case scenarios, I would be the only child, these other having been eliminated or just disappear out of the picture, & then wouldn't everything be peachy she'd ask. What a piece of work this mother was as I said, but speaking of gnawed bones, these little children of poverty and siblings of mine, were going to be getting gnawed as bones by bottom feeders from this local reservoir by carp & catfish, what do you think of mother now? I know that my mom would have totally loved to have turned back the pages to earlier times before she had all these horrible creatures she'd refer to us, but, she was told by Social Workers witnessed by me, that she was just going to have to fess up to the responsibility of her part for having had all us 5 children. It didn't matter to this cat mother what this haughty civil clerk thought about her, she still knew how few of recourses that she had to deal with, the rationing to her would still mean to starve one of us. All the while, all these times that I've had to endure these siblings, satiated full moans the worst glutton of all is this gluttonous mother who after all was the mother cat, and she is responsible for the rest of the litter.

I don't feel ashamed about how I became this Man with the scar.^ let H for homosexual, who felt the compulsion to shock the same way that I was made to have to live with shock practically as a way of life. The local flasher dubbed the ghoul, imagine me being put together with such a gruesome notion, yet when my mother asked me if I was the chupa cabra of a certain town (unmentioned), that I was alleged to being this, by a family member who had been watching me, I only told her, that there was no chupa cabra ghoul, but she had if she would think hard remember that she had thought of me as a ghoul.

I was this miserable mother's subdued and starved, idiot weakling that she had included in her plan to save me by starving one of the kittens, that would be me. I also forgot as a reason that I'm not embarrassed about telling this true life horror story is that I am also stuck with the terrible and dehumanizing defect of stuttering, which makes me appear to be vulnerable. That's the part about stuttering that I hate the most, that this goes along with that mother creating this runtified weakling, from all of her & her other much older son's injuries, literally, & even he could have been made to go to jail for having injured a much younger sibling but (sin embargo), the little sissy needed to be toughened up. One of his beatings nearly left me dead, but I was left for dead too, as he made me promise, that if I ever talked about that severest of beatings that I ever had in my life, that the next time he'd make sure that he'd kill me for sure, so I kept that pent uo inside until I was the age of 19, & this was at the age of 18 maybe, just turned 19. This would be the beginning of a nervous breakdown period that I would get much deeply disturbed and experience clinical depression for 1 ½ yrs. then finally snap out of. This was the time when after 2 quarters at the college I had enrolled in, that I realized that I was truly at a fork in the road so to speak, & I had decided to withdraw from the University life, as this sort of soul searching period was about to take place, along for the search for an actual identity as I felt at the time that I was falling into a kind of abyss, some kind of negative energy that I couldn't put my fingers was making me be under its control. I kept having the beginning of my 1st Post traumatic stress syndrome constant flashbacks to the nothing but abuse that somehow I had managed to not let get to me until now, and brother was I ever in for the disappointment when I was about to realize that there was virtually not going to be any lifelines for my sanity as I went thru this terrible time. Mother would only be there to heap more I'm now worthless again like I always was. She was also about too that I did have a hell of a lot of fight in me when I went into my cocoon, like I had when I had been placed against my will in the

1st. hell hole pit beneath the bathroom, for which I would never so much as an explanation from this torture mother, much less an I'm, sorry. At that same time, I lost more than 20 lbs, and I really couldn't afford to lose 1 of those lbs. My Tourettes, was particularly pronounced this time along with stuttering, and self injury by way of self biting within the mouth, so this mother found this more amusing and pathetic, than some illness that needed to have attention. To the terrifying torture mother this just served to reinforce her belief in the fact that I was her total defective child who needed nothing but severe punishment & neglect, that was all that this type merited. In conclusion, the same mother who had been responsible for the injury to the top and side or the frontal lobe of the brain, which area controls impulse control, now would beset the same child with such vicious & malicious tortures for the entire rest of his life. How do you judge this kind of behavior towards a biological son now?

So, now I go thru life, struggling with all of the defeats & the difficulties that I would encounter as a result of the conditions that the injuries I sustained as a result of having been raised in that family. Sometimes, these bothersome ticks, bites, grunts, & OCD behavior were now becoming, almost impossible to hide, and I have no doubt that the 125 or so applications for jobs had been some of them denied based on these funny quirky defects that I exhibited. I also was up against the feminine factor as I was quite effeminate, but this was hard to almost impossible to hide. My head injuries left me quite diminished, the lack of men in my life had left me with very little confidence, the flashbacks were becoming more frequent, and more pronounced as if I hadn't tried had enough to get rid of these sickening mannerisms, but there was only a meager self support system of my own which I had devised while in the room at the age of 19, that I was able to fall back on, my meditative phase that I had used to get myself out of this clinical depression. From having read a book about the doctrines of being a male, I was actually able to muster enough courage to continue to be placing applications for office work, as I was now about 23 yrs. old, had a son, and a daughter on the way, when a small miracle occurred. I secured a great job working for the govt. as a secretary, and then I later would get promoted to fiscal secretary for a large firm, but I now was a statistical secretary, but still, I was certainly up for the challenge, wow, what a life saver this job would turn out to be for me, and my wife and child and don't forget, there was also my little daughter to be on the way.

I felt as if I knew that I owed it to these poor children of a simple but very loving wife and myself; I didn't want to suffer the terrible starvation, criminal negligence, and the physical injuries that I had, so me and my wife set out to provide these two adorable children of ours a better that we had gotten life, but there was going to be some pitfalls, that I wasn't going to be able to predict.

I did have an inkling that me and my wife would end up tragically, but to try to vicariously relive the childhood, as if in a sense to redeem the horrific like childhood you had, is not the way of going about raising children, and this won't fix your own! Although we did provide a joyous time for my children, this would never make mine right, so what else is new?

Now the hate mother was going to travel down the path of her last and an evolved version of not injuring the body and mind again, but now take the neglect & unacknowledging to her newest level of now adult torture so she proceeded down the "I don't acknowledge your successes and having those children gambit, what a piece of work mother! As a result of this non-acknowledgement of hers, my children would never be left alone save that of once, when I made sure that she knew that if my children were hurt even the slightest way, that I wasn't then going to pay her any babysitting money at all, period, as I knew that I was taking a horrible chance after what she had put me thru, it's a wonder that I even left them with her even that onetime. The one time that I did though, my son bent her fingers all the way to the back which left her injured for a decade, pay back's a bitch, isn't it? I made sure I told my children that if an adult seemed to be guiding them wrongly, to not be ashamed or afraid to show your anger and use force, touché to my son for injuring this hateful mother finally and once & for all! I told this mother right when that happened, that I know that she must have been hurting, or injuring my little son for him to hurt her in this way, but in reality, I was delighted about this turn of events, and I'm sure that this must have showed by my expression of pride that my son had hurt this my bitch of a mom.

NOW THE MOTHER WHO WAS RESPONSIBLE FOR TWO GEN'S HAD TO KEEP HER EYES ON HER BACK

After that, what seemed comical to me & turn abouts fair play, my mother always looked upon my children as something to be careful about, ha ha. Perhaps this is the way that the powers that be in and of the supernatural world are beginning to pay back the brutal torture mother. Nonetheless, even though I had procured a wife & was now a parent, responsible and dependable, the eternal Florence Nightingale matriarch as she sometimes liked to fancy herself, was now embarking down the path of total destruction of the son that she so totally despised, & I can only surmise that sole reason for her hatred is that I was gay, and married. I was can assure, the readers, that I wasn't the only gay man that was having children in this country!

SIN EMBARGO, If I didn't have this bi-sexual or homosexual status that I now so fervently protected and defended, then, I wouldn't have anything much else to return torture to the torture madam that I still had for a mother, but now I myself also embarked on a torture fest, only to return the tortures or surpass them for this mischievous mother figure. For this, I could go back to the flashing/mooning in the hopes that I'd get to her in this insidious way much the way that she was and had been to me & all of my life. I might even do so good as expose myself to one or two, or even many of her so called torture club fiends, yes they were her friends, but they're no fiends to me though. Just why would anyone want to belong to a torture club anyway?

I was threatened with arrest by her and by my sister's as they had caught wind on how I had acted out when all of the torture came back to me in the forms of many flashbacks, of when I had been held in the pit at so early of an age, of how I had sustained a crack to the helpless fragile skull when I was only 2, and yes, the memories of being beaten to within one inch of my life by my older bully brother, & how this nearly fatal beating had been sanctioned by her torture partner, his mother too, mom. All I could think of was, how can I pay these bastards back for how they have made me have all of these nervous disorders, and they not only got away with it, they got away with it and got to mock & make fun of these mysterious ticks, so now they just looked like stupid chucklehead Rednecks laughing at someone's demise, so I now saw this mother like some kind of ridiculous looking heynea that should have known better than ignoring these symptoms of mine but going further & laughing at them!

I should have taken that sledge hammer and hit my head as hard as I could to try to put some sense in this head of mine, as I just didn't seem to get that this mother would never come around to loving this horrible son with all the damages that I had, so basically just would give up on that idea, it finally sunk in, this mother has nothing but fomented hatred for me, and it has to have stemmed from the fact that all of her other siblings were her goose marching automaton—obey—blindly real human child soldiers, but I was not. But then, I hadn't eaten human feces either, probably hers too!

Now, back in the present, I hear the idiots next door claiming that I'm part of their raid, and I better watch what I write, but, I'm still going to be true to my readers, and pay no attention to one thing they say, and these creeps wouldn't know where to start as to how to tell me what to do.

WAS THE ABUSE MOTHER STILL TRYING TO CREATE HER NEGATIVE STYLE OF ANTI SOCIAL FLASHING ANGRY SEVERLY INJURED ROBOT?

The sisters who talked to me about this curious new defect that I felt compulsive about were naturally concerned about their reputation, just the way this dizzy mum was as I hadn't yet developed any kind of reputation. Anyway, this is the way their minds worked, I was still trying to figure how to deal with this constantly being sweaty and swarthy but was only being told that my sex drive had to again put under control, & I guess, this now was a manifestation of how disappointed that I was with the idea of sex! Needless to say, I managed to stay in the area of this sick family that had so hurt me and then proceeded to place the blame on, you guessed it, yours truly. At this time, I would like to interject one of my favorite axioms of the Japanese culture; "One should not concern oneself most with fixing blame, but instead, one should concern themselves more with "fixing problem", something that this mother never would care to do.

It's all I can do to write these wretched lines that somehow actually became my life that I also came to realize is probably the horror story of the millennia in the real true horror stories genre. All my life I strove to make something of myself and all the time I was struggling not to be the like alter ego that I would create with the pitiful thought that I might in some way get back at the torturer's that had actually basically ruined my life by having put nothing but bad memories of the horrible kind in my head, there are basically no other memories, just the terrifying flashbacks.

By the time I'm 29 yrs. old, I'm so fed up with my itinerant employment at best, I've been laid off due to Govt. cut backs, and we had the 1st. of several recessions, the great recession of '72. After hearing such threats from even some of her robotic children, I decided not to listen to them and move far away, so far, that I knew that none of them would bother looking me up especially after the behavior based on severe anger and resentment towards that family. I knew that if I lived far away from these social climbers of a family who so cleverly managed to become popular and prosperous at the expense of starving and abusing one not to mention the severe criminal neglect, then, I wouldn't ruin their lives.

I managed to hitch a ride to a Soughern State, 1100 Mi.'s from this family, & to this day, I have still not moved back. Why would anyone who had been treated the way that such a family treat-me ever want to move back to that kind of a family? Believe it or not, several times they would literally beg and try to encourage me to come back to live near them, only for me to coldly remind all of these abusers how, now I was doing very well, & I didn't want to be treated 2nd. class, be looked past, and not acknowledged, etc, bat they would still continue to try to persuade me to come back, ha, I have them now?

And so yes people, amidst all of these same type abusers, the so called self-proclaimed Raiders heckling, and taunting, that they of all people have also claimed to having gotten my rough draft in their hands, I have to struggle to remember all of this horrible stuff, do these idiots think that I couldn't remember all of these horrible of horriblest memories?

True, I did want to forget all of this since I had already just jotted it down so I was only going to have to transcribe, but here's the joke, I used my own personal form of shorthand for code so that no one else would be able to steal this story of mine, & I think that they are trying to steal this because this story compromises a very intricate, and complicated story or (log line), that only I can or could remember, that if they had the tendency to even want to remember it. I guess that would make the joke on them, ha.

However, much as this annoyed me, this only speaks to how some of the things that I have written about their antics must be true, as they were declaring just at the time that this disappeared that this draft was theirs, and they're saying the same about this preliminary that will go to the publishers. Some mi-minor changes may be made, but you are basically reading the one I'm going to submit, not the one they got, "I wrote this from notes I only could read from that copy." Make that it'? mostly illegible, but whatever they'd get, is all rewritten here.

You would think that if they know how much torture I've endured that they wouldn't even try to use such a ridiculous ploy. Conspiracies abound, anywhere I set up a shingle, but, I see no rhyme or reason in this.

Only my, this final copy will make it to the publisher's desk, or a more finely revised version of this one. Besides, the only thing that this business of stealing this draft accomplishes is to make this tale of all lifelong abuse continue to be true even to this day.

Getting back to I had them, I actually never have them nor would I want to. I know that If I did move back & if I wouldn't be able to get a job, these real true relatives of mine were capable of having me declared incompetent. This final solution of the torture mother & her co-torture siblings, would have conveniently covered up a myriad of inequities on their part. That is to say, one could lock one up again, couldn't they and couldn't one also do this and then conveniently throw away the key?

Now ya beginning to get the picture, of how this actually is the story of a child that managed to survive a whole lot of torture when after so many nervous breakdowns, later in life, the child that is now grown up decides not to take anything from anybody & especially this family or any of the relatives from it.

I literally end up having to escape this Latino woman dominated culture, and I had a vicious hostile aggressive mother towards homosexual or effeminate types in the Mex. culture, we're particularly loathed, where torture's are especially severe in the cases again of the homo's. This mother ties the male organs incl. the testicles with a tourniquet don't forget, & I was that son, don't forget.

The way that I horribly became which appalls me now, was a direct result of all of the above abuses and more. Now I also craved to inflict torture on those who had gotten away with doing what dementedly was done to myself when I was in those tender formative yrs. Only the beautiful consolation & advice with plenty of tender physical touch from this lovely grandma would save me from thoroughgoing demented and permanently too, just like the abusers seemed to me.

Grandma always loved to include plenty of you're the light of my life, and when I had asked her if she could consider me as an apprentice of her spiritual skills, she just told me to stay near her, and just never leave her side. Consequently, I would stick to this cute granny like a sick kitten to a hot brick. I pray also that she had imbued me with some of her psychic abilities. That sweetest of old grandmothers, I have no doubt is what still did sustain me whenever I might have had set back emotionally, she would always be a glimmer of hope & unconditional love that would always be there. On the one hand it felt like my real mother who seemed totally wicked to me by the way that I had been treated, that she was almost grooming me to be her emotional basket case and thoroughly bashed son, but I was forever unwilling to take all the abuse lying down. On the other hand, I also felt that I at least might have a chance at growing up without having this family destroy any chance of a normal life because the sweet grandmother would forever stay sweet on her cute grandson.

Honestly, sometimes were an adolescent infatuated with this truly psychic grandmother so sometimes, I think that we must have come across like the comical movie Harold and Maud about child love and an elder woman, way taboo, but me and granny were truly loving in a wholesome and beautiful way, and we truly were nothing like that. But my grandmother was a woman too, it's just that she was a Victorian so like the Victorians were, she was propheticly prim& most proper. How could a grandmother & a grandson that so nurtured one another not sometimes feel something other than the pure, but we both always made sure we were both thinking with our Jesus in our hearts, what a funny and cute part of my life this adorable relative took over for my mom.

Much of my personality reflects Victorian behavior as a result of this granny's influence. Wow, that was the 1800's & way too long ago for me, but actually if I had my way, I would have been brought up in the Gothic period. Later when I have the propensity to devise this crazy alter ego, as it were, I heap on the dark make up with some ghoulish white highlights to make me look ultra cool and Gothic, as I seamed to feel some sort of remorse at the time & the dark brooding look that this engendered seamed to fit me. After I had began to descend and spiral back to another mental nervous breakdown based on all of the built up pressure from these flashback memories plus current marital affair falling apart, I sadly begin to reach out for all the wrong things as the foundations/bonds I and my mate were slowly beginning to crumble apart. I naturally would revert to my bond that I had long ago made with demon mother that when things would go terribly wrong, due to her poached egg son who never was quite done when I did leave the nest, that there would be hell to play, and t was never kidding about this.

The Ghoul of the Local Big City Was in The Making

But, for I proceed to totally reduce myself & deteriorate any semblance of any personality that I might have developed, I 1st. want to submit to the readers the following exhibit; "I lovingly refer to this exhibit as brain damage (bonk to my head) exhibit, 1-A. (see following page 144 to view injured area to my head and brain, but this mother who probably came from the child torturer from Hades/hell school wouldn't ever give a f'k, much ever care enough to ever do anything about it, that might cost money? Forgive me people for my using expletives, as this bitch of a mother has been deceit for 10 yrs. already when I'm having to go thru this novel writing in this horrible way. Please proceed to exhibit 1-A.

Frontal Lobe Function

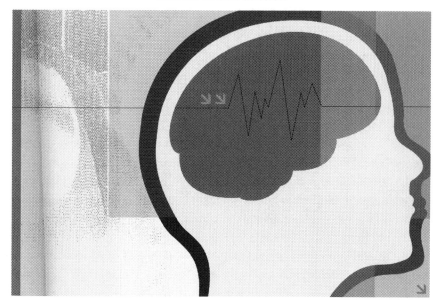

Flash Movie (200k)

The frontal lobes are considered our emotional control center and home to our personality. There is no other part of the brain where lesions can cause such a wide variety of symptoms (Kolb ft Wishaw, 1990). The frontal lobes are involved in motor function, problem solving, spontaneity, memory, language, initiation, judgment, impulse control, and social and sexual behavior. The frontal lobes are extremely vulnerable to injury due to their location at the front of the cranium, proximity to the sphenoid wing and their large size. **MRI** studies have shown that the frontal area is the most common region of injury following mild to moderate traumatic brain injury (Levin et al., 1987).

There are important asymmetrical differences in the frontal lobes. The left frontal lobe is involved in controlling language related movement, whereas the right frontal lobe plays a role in non-verbal abilities. Some researchers emphasize that this rule is not absolute and that with many people, both lobes are involved in nearly all behavior.

Disturbance of motor function is typically characterized by toss of fine movements and strength of the arms, hands and fingers (Kuypers, 1981). Complex chains of motor movement also seem to be controlled by the frontal lobes (Leonard et al., 1988). Patients with frontal lobe damage exhibit little spontaneous facial expression, which points to the role of the frontal lobes in facial expression (Kolb & Milner, 1981). Broca's Aphasia, or difficulty in speaking, has been associated with frontal damage by Brown (1972).

An interesting phenomenon of frontal lobe damage is the insignificant effect it can have on traditional IQ testing. Researchers believe that this may have to do with IQ tests typically assessing *convergent* rather than *divergent* thinking. Frontal lobe damage seems to have an impact on divergent thinking, or flexibility and problem solving ability. There is also evidence showing lingering interference with attention and memory even after good recovery from a TBI (Stuss et al., 1985).

Another area often associated with frontal damage is that of "behavioral spontaneity." Kolb & Milner (1981) found that individual with frontal damage displayed fewer spontaneous facial movements, spoke fewer words (left frontal lesions) or excessively (right frontal lesions).

One of the most common characteristics of frontal lobe damage is difficulty in interpreting feedback from the environment. Perseverating on a response (Milner, 1964), risk taking, and non-compliance with rules (Miller, 1985), and impaired associated learning (using external cues to help guide behavior) (Drewe, 1975) are a few examples of this type of deficit.

The frontal lobes are also thought to play a part in our spatial orientation, including our body's orientation in space (Semmes et al., 1963).

One of the most common effects of frontal damage can be a dramatic change in social behavior. A persons personality can undergo significant changes after an injury to the frontal lobes, especially when both lobes are involved. There are some differences in the left versus right frontal lobes in this area. Left frontal damage usually manifests as **pseudodepression** and right frontal damage as **pseudopsychopathic** (Blumer and Benson, 1975).

Sexual behavior can also be effected by frontal lesions. Orbital frontal damage can introduce abnormal sexual behavior, while dorolateral lesions may reduce sexual interest (Walker and Blummer, 1975).

Some common tests for frontal lobe function are: Wisconsin Card Sorting (response inhibition); Finger Tapping (motor skills); Token Test (language skills).

Additional Material:

- Frontal Lobes and Human Essence
- Frontal Lobes and Humor
- Frontal Lobes and Language Compensation
- Two Brain Areas Involved in Doing Math

References:

Blumer, D., & Benson, D. Personality changes with frontal and temporal lobe lesions. In D. Benson and D. Blumer, eds. *Psychiatric Aspects of Neurologic Disease.* New York: Grune & Stratton, 1975.

Brown, J. *Aphasia, Apraxia and Agnosia.* Springfield, IL: Charles C. Thomas, 1972.

Drewe, E. (1975). Go-no-go learning after frontal lobe lesion in humans. *Cortex,* 11:8-16.

Kolb, B., ft Milner, B. (1981). Performance of complex arm and facial movements after focal brain

Now my people, is when I will amaze myself even more than I will amaze the readers, as this is when I will make the readers see just all of the aforementioned abuse can and will lead to such aberrant behavior, that it's now even for me incredible that someone can ever act the way that I did. I learned most emphatically to hate myself, when I never should have hated myself because I was more than anything a loving and caring individual. I insist that central to my demise is this hateful mother's almost nonchalant manner in which she would treat these conditions as not defects, but nuisances to her imaginary perfect world. Any of these ticks, stuttering, were only viewed as shortcomings & defects that would only serve to support her belief that I was next to a handicapped child, which she vowed that she would never be able to cope with. I fell under the category of loser, unachiever, underachiever, & never gonna amount to anything to this mother figure, some mother figure.

I WOULD CRAVE TO MANIFEST THESE TICKS IN SUCH A WAY SO THAT THE MUM WOULD KNOW THAT THE INJURIES HAD COME FROM HER

And yes, the ghoul she had bragged she had made by designating me as the one who'd be beaten to within one inch of my life on more than one occasions, had made me 60 lb. weakling appearing, was in the making alright as the PTSD that would never be diagnosed would become so recurring, that eventually I'd almost not be able to control them. It occurred to me that the very thing that these matriarch seem to cherish, their chastity, could be a thing I would regard as something I would never have or need according to these matriarchs-. Anyway, they would say to me, that to be innocent for me was a pointless idea, that no one will ever care about a depleted reduced wimp like me, how about that? Turns out in the end that the thing that this mum from hell bragged about last as having been her last and final injury to her son will be the thing I use to injure her and their dominant female society. Who would care about my sexuality anyway, and sometimes, I also would show/display an inner hatred for my sexuality, manifested in an ill regard for sex as my sexual organ had been injured by females, and they would then brag about this in my presence, or in other words, right in front of me like my mother's torture club member friends.

I CRAVED TO USE THIS SEXUALITY THEY WERE CLAIMING DESTROYING FOR ME FOR DEMOLISHING THEIR OPINIONS OF SEX AS WELL

Firstly, I could expose myself nude publicly to ridicule my sexuality, and show it off, then later, I would tell this mother that the way that this felt was in the memory of when I had also at the age of 3 ½ had had to run down the road this way to call attention to the abuses that were ongoing and occurring in my life as a tyke. Had I not done this, my tortures and abuses surely would have gotten much worse. This nifty crack to my head that my very own mother had inflicted with a meat cleaver made it much easier to behave this aberrant way, because as it also turned out, this area of the brain is responsible for impulse control, emotional balance *&* well being, it governs control over compulsive behavior, if it developed. I can tell you that many of the mannerisms that developed I didn't start out with, I was the all smiles little toddler of 4 or 5 months, like my grandson is. By god, the little tyke looks like the spitting image of me sometimes, "ha!" That smiles of mine face was about to change at the tender little age of 9 mo.'s or so. In time, I'd realize that it was only myself that I was hurting by acting out in any self-destructive ways. I already had enough negative marks on my record/card, so why would I want to add a whole set of real crazy acting behaviors to make things worse, but then as I stewed and fretted about my state of affairs, I also realized that I too was going to be like her torture member friends, and the whole point became to ruin my own sex further to support their destruction of myself, yours truly, their bashing favorite, mua. Not only was the fawning over the new and only little other boy long since forgotten, but the bashing of crazy little Juliansite would now be taken to a new and highest of levels. Injure the sexual organ of a boy and rub salt in the wound by bragging that it was done to ridicule and humiliate by a torture mother and siblings, as they would brag that they too were responsible thru their "votes" regarding how to control Julian's sex urges.

After this cruel Drackonian deliberate injury where all women seem to conspire against me including my common law wife, I was never the same sexually & when I had reached a sort of emotional maturity, this devil mother & siblings would toy with my wife and I by having her strike the blow to my groin area and penis. My poor wife was threatened with blackmail by my mother threatening to disclose her skeletons in the closet that this wife didn't ever want anyone to know about much less me. Boy, what people won't do to destroy other people's lives!

But you know what folks, I'm as I said when I 1st. started out, all over all of these ill treatments, neglect, & being overlooked, & so, so much for the precious mother's excuses, "his punishment was appropriate for the deed & for the time that it was done in at that time, such punishment was acceptable." But, I know better as the time was the mid 70's.

In fact the time was about 1973 and I had already gone to an actual Ivy league college and taken law so I had already learned that my parent had broken the law more times than I care to remember with regards to the way I had sustained injuries, endured isolation & abandonment with starvation, & the list goes on. But, the entire time that I was being raised, the family would regard these ticks of mine as defects to be ashamed of, and the family did make every effort to hide me and my conditions as again, instead of being treated for this, (IT) would be treated like (It) was a reason that I would bring disgrace to the torture family. Nobody yet knows that I have any of these conditions because I'm obviously not worth the money needed to pay a Dr. & of course we were abject poor. At the time that I develop all of these ticks, stuttering, & OCD mannerisms, these rare illnesses are still in the mystery to science stage. It was easy for all of these relatives to assign my behavior to having become inclined to homosexual behavior, so now what else was there to cling to besides my cute little granny being the real true Florence Nightingale. My granny was the best buddy I ever had, and that's the truth!

Yes, not unlike the self-proclaimed Rednecks that reside here in the state that I'm presently living in, it is much easier to vilify an individual that is homosexual and form focus groups to meet this end than to try to get at the root of the problem. Besides, just like my mother would think, why would anyone want to assist a wimpy, soft, effeminate son who it would be much cheaper and easier to continue to put down, suppress, and as I said vilify anything good that I might have accomplished.

SO NOW NIFTY HORROR NOVEL READERS, LET US EXAMINE THE IMPLICATIONS OF THE PATRIOT ACT AND HOW IT HAS VIOLATED THE IMPAIRED

As you know, these nifty outlaw Raiders surely have violated and abused this so called important new law to protect our citizens of which people like me with OCD, Tourettes Syndrome, PTSD, THIS LAW MUST NOT APPLY TO. Already to their credit, these Raiders that is, is their claiming that anything I own will be raided until the asset is again in the hands of white people or all of the money from such a raid will go to white Raiders, so as to continue endless raids on me until I basically am penniless, but this book should be a surprise to these sorts, as well no doubt be the proof in the pudding as to whether I will be penniless or not.

As you know, these Nifty Raiders are reading this document as it is being written, so what does that tell you? It should tell you that I'm continuing to be the American Native Son who with all of these maladies brought upon me by the Torture Mother is continuing to be tortured by means of the use and abuse of this important new Law and precedent for the protection of our citizens against foreign terrorists, but this Law shouldn't be used against such citizens as myself with such afflictions brought on by the very terrorism that this Law was made to fend against.

After all, I'm the son, the Native son that this mother who became a terrorist towards Native American Son & the system aided this by way of Firstly allowing an infant to sign a document under duress, and should have known better than to sign the wrong document for a social worker.

So subsequently I still end up in the care of Torturer mum, which my whole point of screaming my head off until I was hoarse so that I would be rescued from the horrible cell that I had been put in, but, the White social worker only saw a pitiful darky who she considered more of a nuisance than a victim, so she took my wrongly signed report/document on my not so loving torture & starvation of infant inclined mother, the same one that struck a meat cleaver to her own son's head. Did you know that if she were alive, It would protect her from having to fess up and make reparations to her sorely injured son, me? This is one of the very worse decisions I have made in my entire life, to allow a white social worker to persuade me to sign the document so that I might stay in her custody, this decision compares to when I opted to go in the pit so that an older sibling who I loved dearly wouldn't have to go in there!

I still can remember so vividly and I can see everything so clearly as I write these lines, I can feel it still just like it was yesterday, the look of relief of the sister who was the one that was going to be the sacrificial lamb so that everyone would get enough to eat. Yet, when registering my complaints to this elder sister about these endless raids by I'm sure abusing the Patriot act regularly Redneck Raiders as they so constantly profess in the midst of anywhere I am, this crazy sister said just so glibly to me, "Well, if the racists are treating me so badly there in the state where I reside, why didn't I move back to where they live," which is where I was raised and all that, but to do such a cowardly thing like that for me compares to these cretins getting away with all that they claim that they have tried to destroy for me.

THE CALOUS MISUSE/ABUSE OF ONE OF
OUR MOST IMPORTANT NEW PROTECTIVE LAWS

So here I am a victim of such immoral and vicious child abuse and not only acting out rebelliously and passive aggressively, but the very law which shouldn't even be considered as I'm anything but a terrorist, but I am actually a victim of a terrorist matriarchical society, yet, this law does no doubt get applied and yes, this is abuse of our Justice Dept. arm of our govt. I have to have more torture now heaped on by the very people I loathe and detest the most, the Redneck Midnight Raiders, thoroughly an outlaw group here to a Chicano American native son, wow, if these crazy people just knew how proudly pro-American we Chicano's are, they never would have even dawned to do such an idiotic thing to such an accomplished individual as I have become over the years.

Rest assured readers, that as this novel goes to publishing, a veritable can of worms is going to be opened, and I will not be the person or persons who will be injured by this can of worms.

I did not laugh at the bragging and gloating with much laughter by the person stating that the murder of a teen aged girl had been allowed to totally be forgotten about and conveniently been swept under the rug so to speak. I didn't even crack a smile with regards to the murder of a teen who lived right in these people's midst & they had drove the bus with this girl, I found no humor whatsoever in such a terrible local lore, & this was the way of the South I was told by such a horrible guy that also was snaggled toothed. Bering added to my already accumulated tortures, is the ongoing psychological tortures, such as just mentioned by these creepy raiders, and of course the constant barrage of Fag, Faguh, he's nothing but a fag, I could kill him, etc. day in and day out until, I by the writing of this horror novel, just make them go away. They never had any power here and I will never let them have any power over me or anything I will do in the future. It doesn't matter to me readers, that they're saying he better watch out and be careful about what he writes, I don't care a bit about their rantings, they're already designated as outlaws by our govt. as I have pointed out abnauseum. There's virtually nothing else that these outlaws can do but this meager and anemic kind of hooping & hollering, in other words, I just consider these sorts as just ranting and raving like some kind of mechanism that has finally gotten to its end and going thru it's last throws.

Has it become more clear now that you have read the last few pages just why such a group would want to steal such a rough draft from someone such as I am, and I want to emphasize that no part of me has anything to do with such elements of society, the dredges of such a magnitude that it's hard to imagine that any part of the aforementioned illegal Raiders, (just check with the Justice Dept.) could even be granted the right to perform/conduct (ha) a raid on such a Native Son as I am and from such an illustrious family as I have come from, albeit the horrific family dysfunction, I'm still alive, which is much more than I can say as to the way that they live and never prosper in their lives.

These neighborhood that I bought creeps, have had to stop the chop shop that the idiots bragged about, they had to stop selling illicit drugs, they had to stop with their prostitutes, and etc. Now, I believe that the drug of choice to peddle in the environs is both Oxy Codone, and either weed or even cocaine & even heroine!

ARE WE AS AMERICANS SURE THAT WE STILL WANT TO INVEST IN THE ULTRA DANGEROUS SOUTH WITH THIS BEHAVIOR NOT YET IN CHECK?

Better yet, if such groups (hate mongering groups) will be allowed to get away with crimes against minorities, the black teen, a victim of OCD, PTSD, and Tourettes, why would anyone throughout the entire globe want to come and invest here where I am treated as I have been and am being treated here in the South where I have resided for the past 23 yrs. This is what has occurred in my life! The people of the South in general don't possess the intelligence nor the compassion to understand minorities much less a N' word to them, "why, why would anyone want to help a darkey!" It isn't in' an. This was their most grievous mistake that these idiots to me made.

The racists in general have thoroughly gone under ground and secret, but their crimes against humanity are still being visited upon us minorities, let that be understood and hear me loud and clear, "I for one am not willing to be f'd dry, but I am apt to offer these Rednecks a jar of Vaseline before they'd get a chance to!"

I know you may ask, "why did this guy stay in such a neighborhood surrounded allegedly by all the myriad hate mongering sorts of the world, and I soon realized that this situation wouldn't be able to be changed. Well, in a way, I have a sort of spiritual (not only of a Christianly version), but view and way that I viewed the dire neighborhood, but some things I now know are truly abject hopeless. Just like I escaped a torturous matriarchical society, I have totally left this miserable group of haters behind & I can forget everything about them and their secret societies, ha-ha.

Sin embargo, I still retain ownership, and please look out for the Sin embargo preposition, as I just chose not to live in it is all.

THE PASSION TOWARDS THEIR PATSY Sancha, WILL BE REDIRECTED TOWARDS THE POOR, LITERALLY THE BLACK SLEIGN NEIGHBOR OF THEIR OWN

If nobody else will, then I am going to, then, Sancha will also be dealt with, even she and her offended son thru my flashing will, my readers ought to be able to contribute to the causes that I request for. Remember, folks, I am the worst victim of all of the victims mentioned, as the undermining and the conspiring also is literally going on right now as I write these lines, do these creeps actually think that they might even get this final draft from me, yet, they're still proclaiming that this is what has to be done. That tone meets the definition of conspirators, & undermining subversives to the enth degree.

Now that I am realizing the abilities that I always had from the time that I discovered this god forsaken neighborhood, this is the handy time for them to intervene to as they have been saying since my rough draft disappeared, we have to take his successfulness away, it's how we learned to be superior torturers. Mostly anecdotal info, is all that was contained in the rough draft much of which I can and have already included herein. Just the same, I feel that there is much that I have not included here, so I will sadly have to conclude this part <u>I</u> and say to the readers that the following part <u>II</u> will be brief and basically cost approximately ¼ or even 1/3 of the part <u>I</u>. The second part to this horror true tale will be much briefer that this one, but don't be surprised I do crank out a lengthy one but, I'll try to keep the price as I said just the same.

You ought to stay tuned in to find out whether the puny trailer park owners who also own a whole bunch of other concerns or businesses that is, take my valuable antique trailer or not, or if they decide to have compassion as they already knew that my dad died & he was my only living parent, but then again, they do seem to worship money. I could tell this when the trailer park mgr. that runs the park for her brother & is where I have this antique placed mentioned to me a Chicano the Baptist church man that she listens to on Sundays & she made sure to pipe in to me one time when I was paying the rent, that her minister supports immigration reform at a time when totally negative extremist legislation was being proposed.

I do not know just how much money this story is likely to earn, but I am dedicated to compensating a good part of that to any person that will prove virtually beyond a shadow of a doubt that this aberrant behavior which is a direct manifestation of the aforementioned injuries by the torturess, my very own mom in turn caused the injuries. I know it's sorry to ask for donations from the readers, but, actually, in a very real way I do not feel accountable solely for this ill behavior, but I believe that the deciest torturess mum is! She must be burning in hell.

I know that by the writing of this, I will threw a shocker & some kind of wake up call, and a realization that the Mexican American of the United States are also human, not unlike anyone else, and can also be victimized by aberrant ill informed parenting. it is submitted by me, that now this I pray showcases a newly re-discovered writer, that is, I now am realizing that I am capable of writing and earning a decent income & I have much more to write.

Hey folks, the fight ain't over yet, and I am still the same vivid man that my grandmother raised notwithstanding the child abuser bio mother who found it easy as pie to divorce herself from what might have been a beloved son. My closest friend thinks that my mother suffered from mental illness, "no kidding", but, if she possessed such abilities as to be able to tutor her other son in advanced algebra, I wonder if she would have been mentally stable or just way too diabolically smart and herself suffering from her own flashbacks of her nightmarish own. Whenever my mom would go to torture, she would have eyes that got empty, it was like trying to make your favorite little pet try to remember you after he had lost his mind to rabidity due to rabies. No matter how I would attempt to try to reach her, to make her see I think I ought to be able to jar her memory, but she would always have the empty eyes of a wild animal that cannot understand humans.

When the sulphuric acid or lye I was made to swallow by her demand, or she would have poured it down my throat herself burned, and I convulsively regurgitated this right in her face to see her also run to the sink and rapidly rinse this off, then, she had her empty eyes.

In the next book it wouldn't pay anymore to keep making the torture mother sweat from my behavior that is the self-destructive flashing, sexual total overindulgence, based upon the torture mother's final blow to my sex organ, to the end of ruining her loathed son which leads to redirecting my torturing back to her in this and any other way I could think of.

I was searching for the sensations that I had had before on my penis for the rest of my life as this mother had seen fit to in a sense anesthetize my organ by the way that I had had the delicate tissue kicked by the wife in that ultra cruel way that my mom knew how to hurt the most when it regards torturing. This was my main fury that I was forever stewing about, then the constant flashbacks that were frequently triggered by this or that event that might occur. I didn't know that I was having responses to horrible/terrifying flashbacks, but then I also had OCD, with Tourettes, and I had to work three jobs to make ends meet & even have a modest living at that.

This story can be considered as being written by a person who might be mortified by his own behavior, but, I'm not, & you want to know why? The persona's that came out or you could even say came on me were in every instance attempts to survive in what my damaged perception from having the frontal lobe damaged no doubt, at least from what I have read as I have been composing this book to survive terrified just like I was when I was being tortured when I was an infant. Only now, the torturing is not only the torture memories by mom and brother and father even, but now the tortures were my good racist neighbors telling me that I was likely to be the next murdered victim from racism in that neighborhood.

The sensations to the organ would return but I want to talk a-bout as to when & how in the final issue of this 2 part book of which we have the racists to thank for having made off with the 1st draft. The moral to this story should be that crime really doesn't pay as proven by my having completed this book in spite of their antics. Crime doesn't pay with me, as I now still own the majority of this diminished neighborhood. I had to close my little park down due to their peddling prostitutes, drugs, and any other illicit crime that they could think of. I downsized that neighborhood singlehandedly. It got way too corrupt for me & I saw the writing on the wall, soon someone was going to go to jail for allowing such a criminal neighborhood to get into such a decline.

IN SPITE OF HOW ABSOLUTELY CRAZY THE U.S. HAS GOTTEN RECENTLY, IT'S NOT OK TO LOOK PAST GROTESQUE CHILD TORUTRERS

It's not OK to look past little children who are suffering from torrid abuse the way I was in that pit! This I particularly have to emphasize to these Southerners that are pursuing the totally wrong angle & going down the wrong avenue. This part of our U.S. esp. is overran by Organized racists in all of its nightmarish forms so that their Raids are unfounded & solely based on only vengeance.

I am making this right, thru this amazing revelation I am having after my nervous breakdown ended at age 47. Though it took me 10 yrs. to remove myself from that center of Racism neighborhood, but then I am a Chicano & just like this neighborhood promised they would constantly try & undermine any attempt of me & my Co-owner to prosper as they were jealous of us being the owners. They also added that the neighborhood would never accept us. They truly were creeps, and vagabonds who lived in the surrounding area & were carrying out their constant tampering (raiding) of our plumbing infrastructure, our electrical infra[1], and naturally, our electric was being stolen too by these redneck thieves, and they warned you that they would too! We were told their racist mottos were: "to destroy their minority opponents, you use their money, their equipment, their rents when possible, & this even was done often as our rents came short way too often, and it usually turned out that these slummers from the area, had used duress to extract cash from my renters. Their racial racist ways also mandated them to act thusly as they knew thru reading Nazi literature I'm sure as I have read this dreadful stuff also to find out how these creeps minds worked. These tactics would normally work well & we would falter a little, but then we always planned for this to offset them, so we always set aside money in reserve just for such occasions, ha ha! We prospered quite well in spite of these people's ignorance, and obnoxious tactics, Nazi indeed. My then lover and I vowed that we would never let these neighbors get away with destroying us & all of our good works in that neighborhood.

Now when I finally came to from a lifetime of debilitating flashbacks which were overwhelming & seemed all consuming not to mention that the homophobic creeps were piping in taunts/harassment right into our house & telling my then mate, "Pediphelia's OK," and to go after my son is OK too, & they'd add, "look at what I was doing," so they would encourage him. To break up powerful land owners, and developers such as me and my partner is also in keeping with Nazi disassemble powerful property owner's structure.

This tactic would almost work, but then almost never had a home just like I can't didn't have a home. Their problem in this case was that we just owned too much for them to destroy our rental income. Sadly again, the joke was on the impoverished racists. It is my firm conviction, that this was when these malfeasant racists would turn to the moderately prosperous trailer park owners to use their wealth to further their racist cause in the area close to familiar environs.

BELIEVE IT OR NOT, SOME WEALTHY TRAILER PARK OWNERS IN THIS STATE DO AND WILL COOPERATE WITH ANYONE OR IN ANY WAY TO OBTAIN MORE INCOME PROP'S

Enter possibly the trailer park where my 1956 Zimmer trailer is situated. The creep who has always been at the bottom of many of our problems, now has warned that he was going to contact other trailer park owners to convince them that fags plus Chicano's shouldn't ever own such businesses, so I strongly suspect that the ones who own that trailer park are behind much of our undermining. The idiot, even bragged subsequently that these owner's were Red's too, so I guess that means, that this is who they must be! The very ones who I had urged to not let me get behind rent on the 1st. home I placed there, now were possibly after my park!

I thoroughly know this mole like guy that is surely at the bottom of all of this mixed up mess, and I can hear him bragging to them now, "I can get you that trailer of his, since your mom seems to think that he doesn't deserve this either." The mother also is an owner of a trailer park too! That mother is now into her 90's, but, just like I have always said, you can't trust the elderly here in FL either, they're the worse ruthless ones in the whole state, and they probably should be. At one point, the brother of the manager were the aforementioned antique is, who is also the owner of the park was highly interested in purchasing my land or my little park, as he is from those environs, but this never gelled. In the past this site, I own has been referred to as (The Nazi's secret Site or Hollow), but then if this were that, I wouldn't want to have anything to do with it. Whatever this property hay have signified, I just own it and don't really care about any of that. Sin embargo, what I do care about is that, an old trailer park owner vilify me, and say such things, in the hopes of taking a dream to me of owning an old time highest quality antique from me & acting like an old helpless, dispossessed withered oldster. That wouldn't fool me. I didn't take anything from her and I don't want to take anything from her. That oldster by the way comes from a time when people like myself are regarded—naturally as inferior to the white man, but I never paid any attention to any of that. Also, and I particularly want to emphasize, never did, never am going to & I never will, it's simply not in me.

Don't you think it would be so easy to sway these also Pro-Red sorts to dispossessing a self proclaimed Chicano, as I feel that this very word connotes rebel to them, when it connotes anything but rebelliousness, in fact, to be a Chicano, you have to have been born in the U.S. and be a super high achiever, or, in the Chicano culture, you're going to be rejected.

For sure, these cooperating Reds have designs on any of my passions, and further, I wouldn't put it past them to stooping so low as to abuse such an important new law as the Patriot Act.

So, now, I guess it would pay them or serve them well to regard me as some kind of rebel, based on the breakdown of my distant past so that they might conveniently obtain what I have worked so hard to obtain. it's funny, how when a person works so hard to forget the ill behavior of the past such creeps in the present that have no idea what I have been thru, just want to do nothing more than to remind of just how ill one can become. I realize fully that the home appears abandoned, but, I have every intention of paying up the arrears as soon as I receive royalties from this.

So enough about the acquisitive ones that want to take my last possessions that I left as my personal effects in that old home.

THE PEDOPHILE DOESN'T GET TO ME BY AGE 46, SO I TAKE A NEW LOVE

I then met a great new guy that promised never to treat me in this way & never has, to talk to me at the moment of orgasm about my child & how he and I look, & he does pipe in the word sexy! But, don't forget, the neighborhood that we (old boyfriend) lived in had caught wind of this lover's interest in pedophilia, so they naturally played heavily on this. Wow, what a world, when all the time I had been with this one, I had always warned him that this kind of behavior of his would be what would be the end of us.

That time when I had to suffer this kind of torture, how would you like to be at the point of orgasm & being with a homosexual lover or whatever kind of lover, and be shocked like that, wouldn't that trigger flashbacks of torture? Don't you think given the conditions that I was living under, it could have and should have? But, you know, Chicano Native Son isn't worth paying a doctor to try to find out what it is that is wrong with him. I went from enjoying sex to being tortured, and by a lover & this is when he would cause painful sex if I did have an orgasm, he would make it painful, because he would squeeze so hard when I would do the blow out, that I suffered for many years after we broke up. But, after he talked the awful way he did, we were over within a few days. He literally came begging on his knees for forgiveness so that I would not leave him, but I would just ask him to get his things and find another place to live asap, as If he tried to spend a knight in the house with me, I wouldn't stay in it, and tell the police everything that he had said to me which I knew is illegal. When this pedophile lover would bring me to the climax and then ruin it totally, I then bolted right out of the den or bed, get dressed tear out super sexually frustrated and this fueled the alter ego persona's to act out in the most self destructive ways that I could think of; there was the Gothic brooder, there was the Clown, and then there was the psycho-lewd flasher who just at that particular time dared anybody to try to shoot a naked sperm hurling self destructive self loathing male nympho, I just wanted to offend the world back like the way I have been offended & especially offended with injuries, however, I decided that I would never injure a single living thing as in killing, raping, or any such thing, I just wanted to shock the way that I was being made to always have to endure shock, and injustice, and nobody cared about me or my sexuality anyway. yes the mad hatter of the famed horror classics I wanted to become, only I just wanted to be able to induce shock, so that whoever it was that I might cause to experience shock might know what It meant to be in shock so that they might feel this way too, and then just let's see if they might like it. I now was in shock as a result of the pedophile who coaxed me to want to try to think as a man who has had a son, yet could be able to actually think of his very own son in a thoroughly incomprehensible way to me & I cannot even get myself to put it down on paper, but the words are in a sexual way! I looked so forward to having a son, but not to think of him in this way, in fact, I barely ever talked to my kids about the subject, but if I did, never in such a horrible way, & I will always be there for them throughout the rest of my entire life if they can learn to understand just how disturbed the human soul can become.

One of my more demented persona (alter ego's) I did develop was the Scarlet Letter naked civil servant, as because I wasn't supposed to be anything or enjoy sex according to the bashes that I had received from women, I guess that was where that originated. The letter was a giant Scarlet H for homo, & I should have been made to wear it around my neck for have wanted to enjoy sex at all. Although it was never outright said that I shouldn't enjoy sex, the injury that I had received seemed to make it clear that I had now crossed these, the women in my life, the line when it comes to how I must have regarded women in my life now. I was very abrasive now far more than before I had received this injury to my organ and my soul, this is a chakra of our human makeup according to eastern beliefs, thusly this organ is also connected wholly to the entire body. According to my mother, I had now received the TONGOLELE, ha!

Now I was going to return the favor with a TONGOLELE, with a PUNGADINGA added for good measure. And now, ladies and genitals, and I think that for all intensive purposes, I had now also slipped into about as many different personalities as Carter has Pills, i was about to make my debut as all of the personalities I had mustered to defy this system that had violated my entire life, and now in the south I am experiencing everything from entrapment, and not being properly legally marandized, and the State was about to railroad me & this state is famous for this, but most especially for blacks or Mexicans. Never you all mind all the inequities of my past thru all the injuries that I am living with without diagnosis.

This state just saw a darkey, and proceeded to try to railroad me on all of these bumblings that had been done in my case when I feel still, that I had blatantly been entrapped, and there should be no doubt about this, but, I will divulge about these incidents in the next and final book as I now have to wind this part to a close so that I can rush this to press then I should have the last part by May or June of 2012.

The darkey that was going to be railroaded, also had a trailer park, and several other assets, and it surprised the jail that I was quickly swept to on the 1st. day after sleeping in a jail with many known criminals. The second jail it was at arraignment, that my partner had posted bail for me by putting up the deed to the house. During the 1st. stay, I virtually got hypothermia & had asked for a blanket but I was sneered at & none was provided & I only had on one pants, and shirt, but they didn't know about when I had been kept in the pit, one of the damages that it did to me was make me super vulnerable to cold, so I almost went into anaphylactic shock from the trembling. I also think that if they would have known these things about me, they still just would have regarded me as just nothing but a darkey to railroad, what the F' would they care if I owned assets or not.

At this time, I am particularly manifesting the symptoms of the Tourettes, & a little more OCD, but, as you know any flashbacks that might come up, I quickly must recognize and also quickly summarily dismiss. This happened as I had been made to have to recall these horrible events of my past due to the Racists who are claiming responsibility, it has always been their goal to induce me to have flashbacks, breakdown if at all possible.

Well, it's not at all possible, at least not anymore, after it has taken me an entire lifetime to come to the understanding of why I chose to act out in the most psychotic way that I ever had.

As I wind this sad sad story down, it just tears me up, that I actually allowed these malfeasants of malfeasants to get over me one last time, "as they brag," but the disservice that is done here is made up by me in the final sequel to my true life horror story.

On them you can only count on continuing to harass & try to prevent me from getting this book published as you already it implicates these sorts in a terribly negative way. They have heckled in the wrong way, in a way that only lead to trouble for them thru this piece of literature.

If a certain law group who lent money so that I wouldn't lose this, my most important asset it ends up were conspiring & cooperating with the surrounding neighborhood so that I would falter also, thereby leading to the property conveying into these lawyer's hands or the conspirators from that neighborhood, perhaps, by the last issue of this book, this will be revealed, only time will tell.

All of my assets, I tried my hardest to liquidate, due to the political gamesmanship of that neighborhood. Bluntly put, the murder of a Black teen's being bragged about, and hearing bullets hurling past my head! Would you stay in that?

As much as I would like to think that much of this is too incredible to believe, the parts about the organized racism & how these practically functionally illiterate sorts are capable of injuring such a relatively large business thru constant raiding, yet just this morning, I woke up to their threatening, that they were going to have to raid me yet one more time, and they sounded so exhausted at least it was the way that they said it, it just sounded like finally and at last they were at their wits end, ha, I bet they are!

THE VERY CREEPS WHO PROBABLY STOLE THE DRAFT LIKE TO THINK I AM AT A LOSS AS TO WHAT TO WRITE, I'M NOT

It's my book, & I'm only going to have thru remembering all of this morbid stuff is all & the worse that can happen, but I now have my pillar, my lover, who always likes to remind me of how he is and always will be there. Don't worry people, I already had made myself go thru remembering this once, and I didn't come apart, & I at best have only 10 pages to go to finish this the most arduous part, and the longest one.

Part of Tourettes syndrome is very convenient for these sorts, we suffer from a propensity to tell other about our defects which to Racists, it is a God send & in this case they have used this to the point of absurdity. This was no doubt knowledge that was absorbed by the Southern Rebels via their Nazi connections. I learned by living in that neighborhood 16 yr.'s or so that the ways of these devils is to hone in on the weaknesses of your opponents & then proceed to use them against him. I gave them OCD, TUERETTS Syn', & I even thru in PTSD, Post Traumatic Stress Syndrome for good measure. I was to them an inferior race, ha, as I was Chicano, ha ha, but to top it off, I also would give them that I was a Homosexual, "Oh, Gow, you couldn't be."

I was firstly thrown back by the loss of the stencil draft, but then I was in fear that remembering again so I could write it down might trigger psychosis & thus psychotic behavior again, but then I really tried not to get mad or any thing like that as that is usually how it 1st. starts.

People, you should be happy to know that I only got close to having psychosis once & as I said earlier, I am not mad about anything accept this lost stencil that I needed to write this, but I was ½ done already anyway, so, no skin off my back.

SO THE RACISTS NEVER DESTROY US AS WE'RE STILL OWNING THE AREA

These villainous Racists so willing to excuse my behavior as typical Fag behavior have now found out that this behavior wasn't just so easily excused away after all. Yet that taunting, heckling & harassing that was going on then and is still going now here as I write these final lines & they're also still reading these lines and constantly commenting on them, as if this would matter but they also suffer from the propensity and defect of telling on themselves, do they also suffer from my afflictions? But, I was about to say that they just interjected," "I hate him, that's just why we so hate him." At the time that was the near end of what I call, "My silent nervous complete breakdown in to just a wide variety of highly manipulating complex personalities that would basically make me feel like I was invincible, and omnipotent, and not willing to be completely controlled. I and only I would be the only one in control. Sin embargo, (Nevertheless), if these any of the suspected few end up with any deeds to my lands, it will also no doubt point to the illegal methods, (raids) of my properties for the purpose of obtaining them. It also is then saying to the world that it's OK to (raid) native son, Julian you know, the one from the (TORTURE HOLE), the one that I lived in with no light, on dirt, with only water and cartilage 6 mo.'s, that one, as my mom would refer to me & esp. don't think that, like my pitiful brethren thought, "I just want people to feel sorry for me," That's the copout allowed to be used against me to reinforce that I would be so pitiful as to always try to place blame for my defects on the parents & siblings. That is to say, "To try to excuse away my complaining about these defects I didn't start out with would become the norm." Besides remember, I was after all nothing more now to that family than "hotito," & snubbed.

Now that I'm an adult and I can speak as I please, "I put such behavior such as the snubbing after I had all of the "punishment basically cause these insufferable ticks, and stuttering, & etc. as the same as the pitiful neglectful torturer mother's statement, "they always want to blame the mother if the child isn't perfect," but actually all of my injuries were brought on as a result of this mother's grotesque abuse and criminal negligence especially in terms of starvation. I must have been experiencing some form of rickets, or scurry or something drackonian. One of those diseases that came about in the 17th and 18th. centuries, only this was the 1950's & 60's when I grew up in this mixed up mess only to grow up and even get old before I would ever be able to figure this all out! I really don't want to be a prolific writer with a Pulitzer prize writing ability, I really don't have that, but I do have a brutal childhood story that I am going to say almost managed to end up ruining my life, to offer as an interesting survival saga that speaks about countless torture memories & these accounts are so interesting, that these memories could probably last a lunchtime, ha!

In fact, I could go even one step further and suggest that I guess that having been able to compile this book anyway even after the outline of mine was ripped off by these braggarts, "you could say that this makes me something like a legend in my own mind, but certainly not in theirs. Although, I probably actually am in their minds (legend that is), come to think of it, I'll probably become a Thelma & Louise types legend after this book becomes disseminated.

Watching the 10/20/11 season when there's plenty of zombie & walking deceist ghoul movies galore, certain memories flashbacks that normally could have triggered terrifying acting out against society at large for having all all of this to come about, society at large for having allowed all of this to come about & why hadn't there been any safety nets for this queeny native son? But what watching zombies walking about during this Halloween season does also is remind me of when I was near death from mostly starvation, but also from starvation for love & which would be many years before the Granny would step up to the plate to be a parent. During these near death times, I was already trembling involuntarily to the point of using what little energy I did have, so I just tried just not to die & not to tremble anymore. I had to contemplate on my death at the early age of 2 to 3 yrs. old, but after I had grown in the pit about a couple of inches, the torture mother would succumb to a health Dept. investigation. The things that horrify me now most is how at such a little age, I was made to have to think about such things as the end of my existence. This also was the mum has managed to make a human ghoul thru starvation with torture of darkness & isolation in spider filled pit & I did have to watch out for the mice & rats too.

I decided that however long this idiot was going to get away with doing this to her own son, the crazy lunatic, I just didn't have a choice but to take it, or risk more such things as almost lethal strikes to the head, or bone cracking injuries by an older brother, or more genital tourniquets!

I had to disobey one who had tricked & lied to me so many ways which put my life in danger in a whole variety of injurious ways. To make this more able to understand, simply put, I wasn't willingly steered, led like a helpless lamb to the local reservoir in my Sunday best clothes either just to be drowned along with all the other four monsters.

Yes, this torture mother that would push the envelope with a mere toddler as her (given to her by the health Dept) real true human guinea pig, would brag to many that I merely represented this to her, and her scapegoat, and that she had almost managed to create her own little ghoul that almost didn't even have to eat how handy! After so many abuses from virtually the entire family what with being the youngest of five, this made it easy for the group to view me as the resented eating machine, constant complainer, and a nuisance in just about every other way as I now was living with a whole host of undiagnosed manifestations from these abuses which usually only served to make my siblings laugh & the mother only seemed concerned mostly with her own reputation, "was this going to come back to haunt her, you bet it was.

Now I live in a different kind of hole, one created by a miserable group of low class scoundrels from the South, here I'm surrounded by them just like I was told that I would be if I continued along the path of continuing to own the property that I do still own, I live in a small 4 apt. bungalow, that is surrounded by most of these crazy Red's as they claim, son's of the South, that are claiming being the ones that are compelled to carry out a "Raid" on me. Submitted by me, is that no Southerner would like to be regarded a native son and have the horrible atrocities that these I know have committed call themselves Sons of the South! If that sort is a son of the South, then as late as 1988, sons of the South murder black teenaged girls for talking up to them even if they live right across the street, even if they shared the same bus ride, you just don't talk up to certain Niggardly white sorts in the South at the time.

Do you think that I'm like this girl who was murdered in the neighborhood because she defied the local yokel's, well, I don't think I am. Although, I have a car wrecked and the culprit who caused looked me right in the eyes, just before fleeing, as to say to me, see, we can get you! At the time, these threats were the what I thought were empty threats, yet this did come to be, & I now have no 99 Ford Taurus which was my best car of two at the time. Even this kind of threat that I live under doesn't and hasn't phased me from completing this novel, such as it had to be finished. Don't forget, we owe that to them, but I'll make up for it.

Right here is where the bucks stops, I stop all superfluous wastes of our strained Govt. funds for such absurd & ridiculous unfounded grounds. These useless raids, "If he didn't always have to be self-proclaiming that he's a Chicano, but then what the hell else am I supposed to claim that I am, if I'm nothing but being a proud U.S. citizen who has to be a super achiever or sink, and that my friends and fiends is the definition of a U.S. Mexican American that out of necessity must outdo his piers, or at least achieve the highest marks possible in his or her studies. But nooooo, down in our old South, miserable & wasteful Raids against minorities is alive and well, & especially ones where networks that are all over the place in the South are more than willing to quote unquote, "perform such so called Federal Raids," I bet the Federal's from the South would do such a thing to (The Native Torture Son of The Millennia). Leastwise, that is what these irritants of my life almost daily claim, that these sickies are actually part of a Fed. Raid!

TO MY AMERICAN GOVT. I MUST ENTREAT, TO NOT LOOK PAST SUCH A SON

So, I the untouchable of that torture family, has at least made it far to have the capacity to figure out my own problems from injuries, and to make the come back of come backs. I'm that American son who broke down here in the South with nobody caring to do anything about accept perhaps, aim verbal pot shots, or actual real bullet shots, the Rednecks, and the Raiders I know would.

Were it not for the constant touch of my Victorian grandma, & her constant reinforcement that I was probably the most loving one of that godforsaken brood, then my behavior might have been much more terrible. How does setting off a nuclear facility by my psychic elemental energy that I know that I generate sound? I did experiment on a recent occasion when I in '08 went to Ohio for a funeral, to see if this could work from so far away and 2 people were killed in this experiment of mine as the storm that I focused on occurred just only specifically pinpointed right where I had wanted this to hit, as this was where I suspected was where all of my problems were stemming from. The place that I was when I was focusing this spiritual energy from was 1100 mi's away, now do you believe that these things are possible, for sure, this has settled whether I could affect this sort of elemental fury for me! Do the readers remember my super genius cousin who at the time before his "accident," was a leader of a band that performed gigs at age 11, he was the class president, he was also track star, but he ridiculed me along with my own brother, & do you remember how this infuriated me one time too many, and now he's confined to a wheelchair for life, at this time I was only 15 yr. old & I think I already managed this.

WHY WOULD ANYONE WANT TO F' WITH SUCH A NATIVE SON

If the reader cannot discern thru all of the grief that so miserably has been visited upon me by way of a sordid childhood of torture & deprivation & including human trafficking by the one who is supposed to protect you, then is that any other way but to spell it out even more bluntly. Well, then, I've said just about everything legally I can say without causing this book to be rated something like an XXX rated book, and that would definitely hinder the publication of this torturous and maniacal account of the most illegal kind of parenting that exists, including potentially child rape, starvation with dark pit accompaniment, once a day bathroom right, cracks to the infants skull, and the list goes on to the point of abnauseum! Fagots ought to get this kind of lot in life, Sin embargo. So, in that spirit, & in the light where nothing would ever be done to rescue & fish out such a Native Son from such environs, I have to state that the final and forthcoming issue to this hideous treatment of our United States Children will have to be getting a rating of at least 2 X's if not have to be rated XXX. Now then, the next section just might make your eyes roll around like the ball in a pinball machine, or at least roll up in your head at the sickeningness of what happened to me, & so now, people, be prepared to learn about the rest of the torrid story that I was made to have to bear in a truly reality sense, this is not a reality based series, but my real true horrific moments that I have overcome and survived.

AS THIS STORY WINDS DOWN, WAS THE VILLAGE I HAILO FROM COORECT ABOUT THEIR SECRET SITE IN THE SOUTH, DID I OWN IT?

It was alleged that a colossal Nazi Swastika was embedded in the direct area of this little trailer park of mine, & is this why I have been harassed by all of their assorted hate groups?

I was told by piers since I was about 10 to 11 yrs. old about a site in the South that would put to death anyone who might speak against Christianity or not espouse Christian beliefs, & this included killing what, "they," considered heretical homosexuals. I am also told that I needed to read my bible and I would find out about it, however, I just might have stumbled upon this site of their superstitious absurd belief. Even if there was credence to such ridiculous notions, I'm just the sort of homosexual that would defy this sort of ignorance face on and inform all the authorities about the wrongness regarding a Swastika in the 1st. place, then proceed to have this destroyed and/or dismantled and speaking of god, with the best Godspeed that any authorized American authority could muster, if such a site were actually in existence & in this country that would have represented a slap in the face to any Patriotic American and an affront to any U.S. citizen. The Nazi Reich rises again, ha! The hate mongers as I set up residence in this forsaken area of the South would tell me that Southerners were against the attack on Germany, & that they were instead more happily involved & this was their example of America's being defied & this was going back to when the South had lost the war on Slavery, can you get a load of our Southerns thinking in this way.

AND NOW, I MUST ASK THE READERS, IS THIS MORE PSYCHIC GIFTS?

If there were such a site, I have now found out about this indirectly, but, I haven't really ever read the Bible entirely either. I did retort to these piers when a little boy, "I think if your religion has such a site, I'll never go there for extermination, but maybe, I'll find it and buy it thereby putting such a notion to rest!"

HAD I FOUND THIS FAMOUS SITE OF THESE JEERING TAUNTING PIERS?

These jeers of theirs, contradicted their religion to me, "Nigger, filthy dirty Mexican, Lil black Sambo, and so on and so forth was what I got from these little piers when I was 7, 8, on up to about 13, when they started to treat me slightly differently, later as we all matured, I would still continue to confront them about having done this to a what I thought was a potentially gifted pier, but they would naturally only lie like white men had clone in the past so often to non-European types, and they all denied this totally, but I knew I had/bared the scars along with all of the scars that that community had inflicted on me.

To me these classmates represented threats, put downs, superior haughty behavior, but I truly considered them inferior to have acted out in such ways. To have clung to German thinking having come down from the 3rd. Reich, well, after all, they were also decedents of Germany & had also bragged & boast-wrongly to me a proud American in the wrong way, "we are white & naturally, we would defend his, "Hitlers", beliefs," this so appalled me, it just served to reinforce to me that this goes along with my childhood taunts of theirs, so these are the true Subversives, and anti-American's & we, (my family), go back far greater than any 3rd Reich of their pitiful selves, to the Spanish Inquisition, and the Mayan meso American Empire, so what, I'd tell them.

Do you think that this alleged site was a twisted attempt to aid by these German's from the area I hail from to make their world domination come back? Have I managed to foil these malfeasant un-American classments and their wealthy farmer parents? I used to like to tell that I knew about the great American land grab, & that the land that they were grabbing was our ancient burial grounds our basilicas from the Spanish Rule, & much of our Mezzo American also holy sites that may contain curses, just like Egyptian burial tombs, Mexican pyramid sarcophaguses, so they had better learn about the cultures before they might start bragging prematurely!

Just look at what I might have pulled off, and I'm proud to say that I descend from peoples from these environs that have been disposed from my peoples too.

COULD WE AMERICAN'S ACTUALLY STILL HAVE TO SUFFER SUCH BRAGGING? THIS AMERICAN IS UNWILLING TO ENDURE SUCH BRAGGING!

Was I the proverbial torture child that was being groomed to act out in this most hideous way, and I did try to think up absolutely the most sickening and repulsive manner in which to sexually offend as now I had even been brought THE DREADED HIV virus to make things worse, and by my current mate. I knew that there already, that there would be many that would be willing to jeer and rejoice at my betrayal, but, I had to just swallow this & take the terrible new development in stride, so I learned to adapt.

Sometimes, I thought that my mother was in cahoots, or at least wanted to be cooperating with somebody, who I would only see from afar, "these large white women who looked totally Spanish", would surface from time to time. I always suspected these as the cronies that my mom regarded as her beloved torturers that I also believe made my mother feel a sense of redemption as I know that this mother had also been severely tortured as a child, and by her very own father also, why does it always have to be the parent that plays with either a child's mind, or abuse the child sexually?

A male had sexually had his way with this mother of mine who also was a trusted relative & now she would keep a legacy going. In conclusion, 2 wrongs don't make a right.

Now you see I can remember vividly the memories of this tortured childhood because there was no childhood almost virtually not at all so these *are* all and basically the only memories that I do have, that of a missing childhood, one I was told this torture mother that was now over, at 2 ½ yrs. old. Sin embargy, (nevertheless, even a tiny infant will have a will to survive. After my memories from the crib, I was resolved that this mother who had stuck pins above my left ear as if she was searching to find out where the injury point was, or what was the point where I couldn't tolerate anymore, this monstrous mother looked at me as if I was her personal experiment. But undoubtedly her possession, like some slave or object to take her torture, but I refused to do her bidding. This resistance or reluctance was based on common sense on my part especially after I felt a pin go into my head, (need I remind you this was me, not my privileged siblings who were at the time free roaming as I was still stuck in this crib. I had little clue as what was to come, but the meat cleaver to the head which nearly knocked me out, gave me a good idea of what this sick angry mother was capable of. Now I would rarely listen to this so called mom, and I would challenge her on this issue for the rest of my life. How can you be my mother when you can hurt someone who you dare to also claim is also your child?

As I write these sorry lines such things as (the fucker learned to type) I have to hear coming from a (claiming they're a raid) No doubt an illegal one, as usual, merely no doubt because I'm coming out with it, the expose of expose's, that now once she referred to herself as a torture mother too [unable to read] mother's would compare [unable to read] pun intended and for all tells on this torture mother that I often times heard her brag to her so called friends, that I also would hear snicker at her most recent tortures of me, so to those friends of my mother's I also dedicate to "right sherlocks" her friends who laughed as I listened in horror as she would brag, something like, I called him hotito at least 100 times and I know he's one as I am making sure that he won't want to be one after I'm thru with him. Well, I guess I have proved her and her friends wrong as I write these lines, & anyway they're all dead now, including my so called mom. Oh, I almost forgot, these creepy friends are dedicated to these Southern Raiders, Nazi's Skinheads, and the like, they're all affiliated, & all of these absurd hate mongers, I guess this makes me the master of all hatred they so brag about like this toddler torture mother, amen.

To this I consider bitch mother I also am proud to declare I not only have a gay son, but his gay husband that I am prophetically both proud of as well as a daughter that is not and so far just one pair of these couples have given me 2 grandchildren & I look forward to my two sons giving me additional children to love, not torture & ridicule, so much of the proceeds from this book will be dedicated to making this happen if I could be influential in such a way.

At this time I want to interject I not only have[unable to read] such dynamic children, but they (namely a professor of Linguistics) will be editing this manuscript when it's finished & he is capable of interpreting it into no less than five languages, & I'm sure he will do this if I simply ask and pay after the proceeds from the English version comes in.

This is probably the club she was refused enrollment to because she had (Oh has horrible (then) a gay son a "HOTO"

So then, about all that was now being done was put downs, physical pain with humiliation, "the tourniquet", you said, "you wished to be a girl" & just after they were purple and turning black my testicles that is, 'lil sis came in the room and stopped her or she was going to pull on her own designed contraption full force, "the way I knew she knew how to strike like when the strike to my head went, full force, but, I was saved by the bell, or sister dearest who just happened to visualize the mess this would become so she protested, "Don't you dare, you'll hurt him terribly and it hasn't been enough time you know as I watched my genitals as they were so darkened from lack of blood flow.

I was absolutely terrified at 2 yrs. old I'm going thru this! The moral of this story is that a child that was as if almost programmed to be a failure and a forever rebeler against constant abuse, community vilification, and estrangement with constant put downs, yet still never gets Justice as this tormentor master gets to get away with a whole lot of child abuse, criminal negligence, even abuse of an acting as an adult child who has already left the nest as I was 20 when she convinced the wife to injure her then common law husband while in a deep sleep, again the way my mom knew how to trick me best, her vulnerable son, "only when he is asleep", that's how diabolical my mother could be, & I grew up with this twisted mother doing such things to me quite often, I seemed to be the brunt of her jokes, I was her personal living example as to how not to behave or you would earn this kind of sadistic abuse, of a life changing nature.

What I mean when I say my childhood ended when I was in that pit is; there no longer was anything but just a dirt pit that barely was warm enough, there was only darkness accept 2 or 3 cracks in the cinderblock foundation which let in the tiniest bit of light that I enjoyed thoroughly, but that was only when it was day & by night, I only knew solitary confinement but with darkness, this was my daily routine: at the end of every day after the gnawed bones had been hurled at me, I then would only be allowed to drink water, "I gathered, she at least had to do the minimum to keep her prisoner son alive", I also got to pee 2 times that mother dearest came to check on me to let me out to use the bath directly above, then "Rouse", back down the dungeon (really the plumbing from the bathroom above), then slam, the trap door was shut on me, but if I climbed out, I was assured, that I would get much worse, so I had better not try.

There almost never was any No. 2 as I never had any x-tra carbs only cartilage & that's all, not enough to ever have any kind of healthy bowel movement. I too took advantage of the dire state of affairs at these times, although to no avail and I'd say things like, "There never was any meat on those bones and I really do remember that well, so, I'd snipe, "I've seen you polish off what little meat was on those measly bones before you threw them at me, why you ask me to come up there to take a dump, when you know well that I never eat anything. Yet, her response to me was just to smile, and in such a wily way, It only served to reinforce my total distrust of this hellion! I now only regard this so called parent incomprehensibly, and wouldn't you?

I'd often plead to her what did I do, why are you doing this to me, your baby and your only other little boy, so she'd reply, "You're not a baby anymore at 2 ½ to 3, you talk like a grown up and act like one, so I'm going to treat you like one, you're tough, you're like a grown up", "But, I guess I can thank her and the pedophile uncle also named Julian ha ha, for learning about carnal knowledge via his sexual child abuse of me, and I being an idiot child thought it was playful banter, as I hadn't actually learned right from wrong. Nope, I guess I wasn't any baby of your's any longer, thanks to you and your sickening deal with regards to the rent, and I was his to do with as he pleases, remember? though an infant now, these and many other evil flashbacks would be the stuff that these terrifying uneraseable flashbacks would be comprised of: I would have to become an adult with these beginnings of flashbacks of my childhood torture and usurping, I had no childhood except from before 8 or 9 months. This infant's terrifying childhood abuse would hinder the normal development to become this angry monster and although I was tough all of the accumulated grief would finally take its toll. I was led to a nervous breakdown by the age of 19, no doubt from all of the lifelong, & this was only amplified during the most critical adolescent yrs., yet, somehow I managed to shake this by about the time I was to turn 20. Then "condenado", condemned one", was added just when I turned 20, as her hotito she now declared me to be and later she'd add I repeat meant that because I was a gay son now, meant that I now had earned the new title of "Condenado", what an award winning mom!

Did I mention the numerous times I was stretched out spread eagle at about 2 ½ yrs. old on the kitchen table held down by my dad and mom for the purpose of castration but this little child I was didn't know whether this father was capable of & was to learn later that he truly was, after I watched him cut the throat of a goat at the tender age of 13, this goat watched as my father placed a cup by the jugular vein he drank it before my eyes! I had also seen him dress raccoons, rub [unable to read], chickens which that's OK [unable to read] not a pet goat we had named that's crazy & [unable to read] I never got a break from these two hetero parents that were determined not to have a homosexual son, so I forever lived in fear that I might be abducted (snatched) in the night the way my mother had done when I was a tyke! I also felt by then that I would be lucky if I could survive the physical & psychological abuse & didn't yet understand because I only had memories of real bad abuse. I do have to admit that this father was the nicer of these two such parents, but he tricked me as I was extremely squeamish & never would have agreed to have witnessed this, you see they had this idealistic view of the older brother I had who they were still trying to impose this kind of tougher & rugged mannerisms that to be completely honest, I was probably more soft than my sisters were plus I was their baby boy, youngest child! This consequently had a slightly traumatizing affect on me as I still can visualize the terrified wide/bug eyes terrified look on this helpless goat that I knew of all things as a family pet, but its' name slips my mind.

Now these Redneck Raiders at least that's who they claim they are and the voice tones I know to be these sort, are saying "He's going to be found, floating down the Hillsboro River here in Tampa, "Oh what fun I have to look forward to. To that remark, I only have to say, "Just so long as it's not Face Down on the Hudson like Jim Neighbors was alleged to be found, ha, that's an old one.

This father was illiterate and tended to do my mothers bidding, but I watched him plead with her to not perform the castration, so I now know now that he is deceased, that he truly would have done this, had I not cried the way I did. he looked at me the way dogs look at their bitches siblings, like those balls were not something to be proud of the way I was about my son's, but as if my balls were a threat to his prowess, & or his genetic pool, how ridiculous, I did have a giant set of balls, which is probably why I gave them a run for their money, & I mean their entire lives! I am the personification of disgruntled to these two! Yet I had my full dose of testosterone even though I was a toddler!

Believe it or not these malfeasant hate mongers are reading this as I type it and to what end, I am only going to depict them as they are, full of hate, out to get ya, (ha, ha) I also have been trained by a U.S. MARINE that served 2 yrs. (count them) on the front lines in the Tet Offensive, certain guerilla moves, & thru all these yrs. living in the south and being a business owner, I [unable to read] have grown eyes on all sides of my body, I trust no white man from the South! My trainer I shouldn't admit is my very own brother who taught me very thoroughly at the orders of this hateful mother, perhaps this is one of the few things that she and he left me. This brother is still alive, & I honor him for this to this day, he will not only be my hero for life, but he has finally earned my respect forever too! I should add, he trained me until my moves pleased him & he taught me these moves when on furlough from the Tet Offensive, this chokes me up that he had to do this in a foreign land around people that he did not even know much less yet hate. Still he knew he had to train this gentle soft brother to defend himself as his mother/our [unable to read]) had a very vociferous talk with him & ([unable to read]) this brother complied to the point of correcting my hands repeatedly so that my move would be deadly, I can disembowel, I can pull your eyes right out of your head, it's called me or you!

[NOTE[: Editor's notes, please include these lines with page 38's 3rd. paragraph, (it's the writing in the left column)

The reasons that I was myself convinced that my dad could carry out this castration was the way that he would talk with my mother with regards with these gonads of mine. Also I remember this horrible memory when I was tricked to witness many times when he would dress the game that he had caught. Later in life as a pre-teen, I was forced & tricked to witness this brutal dad to an effeminate son to watch our pet goat who we had named be slaughtered. Now, mine you I was under the impression that there was going to be a slaughter, but I thought it had already been done, when he called for me to bring in the meat, but he asked me to bring a coffee cup so like a helpless lamb like the one that was about to be killed idiot, I came to dad with the empty coffee cup. I actually thought dad was probably going to go inside throw some spice on the meat to cook it I know that sounds crude but in our house this is commonplace. But, no, both I and the poor pet goat were fooled. The poor little nanny goat just watched wide eyes along with my wide eyes, as dad cut the goat's jugular vein and as I and the goat watched the cup fill with warm steamy blood, then dad opened his eyes even wider and drank the cup (de heelo) all at once, then he wiped his mouth and uttered, "It doesn't get any better than this!" Now I at least had grown smart enough that I knew better than to protest I suppose I also understood that this was part of my being indoctrinated into the mach slaughter & dress mode of game. "Wow, one later, I was tricked also by my mom & Saneida, a local Mex. friend of the family, only this time 2 woman would dress a little nanny goat all by their selves, what a lil' Chicano's life!"

Such is the life and formative childhood of a shunned, rejected, negl (& definitely have to interject criminal negligence) child that has effeminate tendencies & that had nothing but sisters and a mother plus a grandmother to guide him! My father was either at work, gambling or probably womanizing which probably caused the mother to hate males, even the one she gave birth to, to the point of attempting infanticide on many more than one occasions.

Mom used to tell me that she had books that she used to guide her that told her how to create a family that would be undefeatable, a family that would be comprised of a simply put group of super children & that she was reading these guide books, & that I had better pay attention and never defy her. This mother was the all knowing, could not do wrong by her children & I had better listen well and never ever disobey her or I might not be included in her super children plan to rule the world and not be able to be defied. Eldest brother was tutored in algebra by this genius mother & later also tutored for the advance level, geometry & trigonometry, this brother works for a top secret Govt. top level extremely important & significant arm of our govt. The problem I had with the mothers super children plan was that my super child potential was beat out of me by this torrid child abuse when I was given to an illegal alien uncle (HA) NAMED Julian Rodriguez. (See the super child plan of my mother) I was supposed to be tortured psychologically and physically since childhood must have been her plan for this super child. I remember to this day being able to start fires by placing my hands over a given area and just thinking this & placing my hands over the selected area and fire would start. This I was warned by my mother not to dare do this ever at school or I would be told that I had devil or Satan in me. Because I did not trust this mother I certainly did not believe her so I did do this at the bottom of the slippery slide at my beloved school I attended as child & this was witnessed by these little rather 1st grade peers but I was told that this meant I had *Satan* in me & then one said I had devil in me. Now, I believe that among other talents I remember possessing this paranormal ability. One I distinctly remember enjoying was beat out of me if not only by mother but also my peers but also by wanting to be loved if not by my mother any longer, then maybe by my childhood peers therefore this is why I wanted only to gain friends & was the only reason I started the fire with only the hope that someone might grow to like me & maybe grow to love me. I just know I was much driven by the desire to be loved due to the fact that I now only knew such physical abuse that I was completely convinced that nobody at all loved me & I had been thrown away so many times already that I would have loved and clung to a warm rock if that would have been the only thing available which was about the amount of it, coupled with total maternal love rejection turned to hatred.

This mother boasted to me that I clearly had super child potential but if I did not listen thoroughly and obey blindly I might not make it & I would say you're not reading such a book, "o yes I am", she'd confirm, then embellish that the book told of a mother that ran a government thru her super children & she was able to become this mother. So, I'd retort, I don't want to play this game and I just want to be your little boy you love again. "Oh, but you know how I feel about that, she would say, "you're not a baby anymore, you talk like an adult & so I will treat you like an adult from now on, & just so you know this I just want to remind you from time to time with psychological abuse.

I remember this real horrible memory when I was stuck in "hit me mom so I would know some touch connection," so I'd look forward to her beating me up, to a touch starved infant this at least would mean at long last I had gotten some kind of tough, wow, pitiful! To me it meant at least that I had touch plus a whole lot of bruises and probably fractures, but still I looked forward to the next blow. Just to have any attention would mean I meant something to this creature and now I began to wonder, why did I want this thing people referred to as love and so I would express this to the creature.

This is when mom would come alive and would say some crazy thing like, "You do have courage as you dare to try me on and then she would put up a fight which mainly involved fending off my futile attempts at matricide, but a 2yr. old can hardly injure a full grown adult. What was evident in my mother's eyes was she revealed in the fact that she now regarded me formidable as thru all of this criminal abuse, I had from time to time become rabid, again wow, what an infants life! Yes, she no longer viewed me as the little cuddly baby but it's innocence was gone or so she thought. I was instead her psychological challenge to see what I might become all on my own, without any love or tough at all, dearest mommy, mommy dearest.

Mom sure must have moved to the right neighborhood (German Township) in order to have gotten away with this. Anyway, as I grew up with the piers that I would grow up with, it seems that my piers also talked about the many tortures that they also had endured, but they would tell me that this was just typical German sternness and regimentation, or so they thought & also were led to believe like I was, only by this Mexican American sadistic mum. Mother would like to also pipe in that some of our piers and contemporaries from the area were in complete accord with her antics, albeit, these same neighbors also felt the same way & she would add, "mandatory sterilization was a good thing & you're the kind I think should be sterilized & these good Christians shared her same views, she'd add.

Until my mother's death, well, "put it like this, I did not know if I'd self destruct in which she & the "her Christian world" would rein successfully over me, her gay angry son who just wanted closure which this mother & I use that word loosely, was never willing to offer, she'd only say, "Well, I warned you, and you know, because you were bad, you got what you deserved! The punishment is just for the wicked son, "Condenado", (condemned one, that you were and are, so, always remember me with those injuries I inflicted on your person as lifelong & life-lasting memories of me and why I hurt you!

Such a devil I had for maternal guidance and nurturing! I suppose I could approximate or estimate this mother turned on me and completely stopped the sweet cuddly love I had gotten used to at 7 or 9 months after she stuck sharp knitting needles (as she was a proud needlepoint) seamstress), into my skull above my left ear, I will remember this always, and the images haven't changed, yet it feels like it was just yesterday. In fact, this so angered me that by only the second time after she had tried this, I already reasoned that I'd use my pinpoint 100% accuracy aim I then possessed to hurt her! So at 8 to 11 Mo's old, I used this accuracy as only an angry abused toddler could use to aim at this vicious caregiver mum. I too remember this like it was yesterday, and I pointed the sour and empty bottle at her, straight at her & she was about 8 to 10 or 11 feet away, so I hit the bitch bulls eye right on her head, and it struck her bulls eye. You see, I was not only mad a bout the needle attempts, but I was angry because she was regularly feeding me sour & or curdled milk which had given me diarrhea or the runs, but that sour milk absolutely and did me no good, & when I hadn't gotten the sour curdled milk, I only would get a grumbling growling empty stomach. Of course for having done this if you have been keeping up with this story line, this is what earned my strike with a meat cleaver to my skull, and she snuck up to me from behind after much practicing that I saw from afar, only a little baby that is still in diapers that I still was wouldn't be able to even fathom that a parent could be capable of this, less figure it out!

I suppose this mother having been a great scientist and clinician as she'd brag all her life must have known this area of the brain governed compulsiveness and or ability to control behavior. Later in life as I am now middle aged, I saw a serial killer show on the television which described how injuries to the frontal lobe (the top left and right area of the skull/ brain, could lead to very aberrant and compulsive and obsessive and deviant behavior can and will be a result. The piece mentioned either Dommer, or Bundy. Whoever this serial killer was, it escapes me now, however, after the injury had been sustained by the child victim, the injured subject became compulsive about his murders, and then proceeded to become serf like and their murder rampages would begin. "Was this crazy mother of mine using me as a human guinea pig to create a compulsive angry son for her own angry hateful self and secret agenda which she only showed me to be for her remainder of her miserable life! A quote from this Rose colored Glasses mother, "I have designated one of my children for an experiment and I will use this child for life & they will then become just my experimental test subj. and this position comes with certain perks, such as this child can do anything they want and answers to no one," "this is how she tricked all of us to want to be this lucky selection, but it also tricked all of us to want to be this lucky selection, but it also came with certain drawbacks such as no & I mean absolutely no love from this mother but her hate of this child was allowed/permitted and I should also add encouraged!" Everybody recoiled then, but now it was too late for me, so now I would bear the brunt of this mother's Holy Christian hatred for the entire rest of this child's life.

My [unable to read] in a very small incarcerated [unable to read] for a mother that started out delirious happy to at last have a long waited for son only led to OCD as this Hate consumed mother it seemed to a 2 yr old wouldn't ever love me ever again. I'm sure that our sorry mother began to hate us as her and dad's children when she came to the awakening that this father was a womanizer and was gone most of my formative childhood. I vividly remember when she would say to all of us tender children that she possessed the courage and fortitude to put us all in the car & drive us all to the reservoir all dressed in our Sunday best clothes for the purpose of heaving us all in the body of water and then she would remind us that because we were no longer her obedient children, that this of course would be for our own good. In fact one time after these threats had been made, she persuaded all my older brothers and sisters to prepare themselves as she was going to take us all to a beautiful heavenly place that we were going to be happy at for the rest of our existence, of course all of these bro's & sis's saw a kaleidoscope of possibilities in their tender little minds but I at 2 ½ yrs. old said to these fellow siblings, be careful she's trying to trick you all & she's not going to fool me, so all of my brothers and sisters declined from getting ready for their final demise, so there was no ride to the famous reservoir in Wauseon Ohio.

Recently I had the good fortune of meeting my 1st. grandson who at the ago of 1mo. and about 20days, was happy to meet me & I of course was delighted. At the same moment when I met this beautiful grandson who almost never stops smiling, this event reminded of the innocent child I once was, before all of the sexual along with physical abuse I survived occurred, & this thru me for a loop. I at this time had to contain my inner anger so as not to offend either my darling daughter or my wonderful son in law and this sort of copy of me my darling innocent grandson & of course Baby granddaughter. I only managed to say to my daughter (and this comment was a way out of the way "he reminds me of when I was all smiles too before all of the abuse & near successful infanticide occurred", then I promised to never utter such a comment again ever again and promptly apologized, but I know my daughter forgave and expressed sorrow but quickly changed her composure to one of happy to see her dad anyway as she also has heard me lament my entire life of this torture mothers abuses and unhealed injuries! Sorry again, baby doll, at least I know that you & or your children never did nor never will you suffer such abuse a the hands of your own mother!

At this time I want to interject that this is particularly difficult to write due to this band of horrible Racist Redneck Raiders and Nazi Cell that is hold up next to this apt. as they gloat over these abuses due to obviously that I am gay, so they use this to further taunt and torture, it makes them gleeful that I broke down as a result of these & other of the worlds abuses toward gay people and ones who are very little and in the training course. What did she expect from her very own little baby boy after she had let an uncle by the same name to rape and fool with at about

9 to 11 months! Her legacy of tormenting this son lives on by having named this son Julian!

People, wait till you read later about how this mother, who is capable of all of the aforementioned crimes against humanity in the form of child negligence (criminal negligence, infants prostitution, imprisonment of her own infant, etc. criminally negotiates this child his ability to act out his life criminally. Sin embargo, the child is 16 yrs. old, legally a minor full of rage and anger & she knows has been terribly discriminated against by school & peers yet this mother agrees to allow the child to act as a criminal at this early of an age. this mother that has seen her son have to recover from so much child abuse: I would never hold still, "I had recurring horrific childhood memories with nightmares often which included being tortured & ultimately killed terribly, I lived in fear that mom might steel me away while in my sleep like she had before, "these fears were difficult to shake, these and other memories I lived with made getting over the child sexual and physical abuse not an easy task you know. Now I've developed many mannerisms that are irritating to her, such as, besides not sitting still, fidgeting, I'd bite myself often, the trembling involuntarily has repaired now down to only when I yawn & I still am that way though I do remember that before the abuse when I would yawn I would not tremble involuntarily. To this day I have frequent facial ticks that sometimes I cannot hide but I just live with it. Also currently I still have cuts allover in my mouth from where I bite myself. Yet I know that much of why this accelerated now particularly is due to neighborhood taunters, harassers, and illegal surveillance & while I am writing these lines all of these memories compiled over the years take their toll. I also have to live with hearing this woman's voice read this as I write it, along with this creepy jerky sounding man who likes to finish me and my partner's sentences. Getting to my many undesirable defects my lovely mom loathed she considered me soft and effeminate of course so among all the above-mentioned defects mother liked to single out this one in particular and very often so much so that she thought I grew up with no confidence, but although I suffered from many clinical depression bouts, I still knew who I was, what I was capable of, my strengths and my weaknesses. Yet I still just yearned to just be the loved little boy who the mother abandoned forever so this mother would try to use that this helpless weakened little boy needed just even her to look my way and once give a look or a gesture of approval & or love or affection. To my mother, this was currency, a thing to be bought & the currency she wanted for this love had to be believing her Christian belief's and obey blindly. I was not willing to do this after I had been lied to, tortured, imprisoned in a dungeon, my skull cracked open, need I say more? I am almost 100% positive that the self injuring biting tongue and inside of mouth comes from the time when I would ask for my mom to throw stuff at me so that this would remind me that I at least was connected to a live being such as this mother was, at least I had some kind of hope that maybe one day I just might be out of the pit below the brick school house where we were housed as children even though it had been converted living quarters below, underneath the bathroom was the plumbing crawlspace which doubled as the chamber where mom would take turns placing her little vulnerable children if the were too disobedient!

I have have to make myself forget certain terrible events that occurred to me different times just so that I could go on with the rehabilitation of my emotional wellbeing: "like the one time when after a very long (to a child) @ about 20 months having recovered somewhat from the horrific head wound I developed some kind of emotional stable self concept & I for some reason imposed this identity onto my brown little teddy bear and after I had been discovered as sexual discovery/exploration with little sis, not only was little sis taken away for a year ½ but teddy mom by all accts. just threw my "identity from a long recovery after near infanticide attempt (meat cleaver to my head, teddy bear away and she emphasized this teddy bear was no good for me, that it made me like a girl and things were now going to change dramatically so that I would not stay this way. I went into a tailspin and had to learn to talk all over again, and this took a very long time for a child this seemed like having to start from the beginning over and over again.

If there's anybody out there who thinks I've forgotten the sickening thuds of the times when I was being beat up by a much older brother who was being directed by my mother who praised him for taking over her job & she would make sure that she would point out how it would be pleasurable to inflict this punishment, ha!

Why is it that almost anywhere I decide to sit it's usually alone these days as my lover prefers to sit in his lounge recliner that I bought him, I almost always invariably ended up squashed up in the corner of wherever it is I'm sitting. Is it because I involuntarily regress to when I was in the pit beneath the brick schoolhouse? To me this is sickening too & I always feel as if there is something that compels me to do this because it just seems that I have to cuddle up to the armrest just like I cuddled up to the dirt floor usually in the fetal position, but you know I really hate feeling like this. I guess when you literally have nothing and/or just nothingness, you must just curl up in a fetal position probably a form of severe regression and you could believe how this would lead to total worthlessness and later chronic clinical depression which I know is what happened to me.

No to be disrespectful of an American icon, but sometimes I wish that when I finish this manuscript, "I have a dream too," and hope against hope I were able to hypnotize myself to for get all of these ills that have beset me as in the ticks, inner mouth biting, clinging to corner/nooks or crannies & or thought people just [unable to read] would then just be auto suggested to go away, but rots of ruck! Sin embargo, I'd be crazy not to try to remedy these defects while I still may be able to if I just focused enough.

Sometimes it amazes me that it's really me that is writing these lines because it just feels like I'm up above or something & looking down at me doing this because I have been able to repair most all of these injuries that were performed both on my physical body & my psyche! Still, I can't believe that I got through all of these horrible memories without being baker acted or committed to some asylum but I do suspect that there are still evil sinister people out there that would love nothing more than to see me put away even though I have spent a whole life trying to forget these terrible memories so that I could as I said earlier, go on with some kind of life. At the very least, there's no mommy dearest to critique whatever it is that I accomplish by taking a teddy bear away!

My "I have a dream", goes something like this: I will strive to be able to get thru writing these terrible accounts as I remember them, as my constant flashbacks brought them back to me in a most horrific way & now surrounded by racist rebels who sought to exploit these defects in me for their wicked gains. As it turns out contrary to these terrifying subversive low class white racial types, I've been seeking all my life to try and understand why I was treated so terribly by my family and society but you know the answers has been there all the time only I wasn't willing to accept the terrible truth of why I was isolated from everyone and everything that can make a person grow up to be a normal citizen and be a productive member of society and it was that I got ruined when I was just a tyke and even though I tried with all that I could muster up it was never going to be enough as I had a torture mother who sought to torture her very own child due to the fact that her husband was a womanizer, (that may have caused her to hate males), also due to this itinerantly employed border I was given as if a gift, as I remember it to do with as his sorry border wanted & he did happen to be a relative who was named Julian Rodriguez too. This mother would use this horrible fact to work on my psyche in efforts to tear me down, but I was too tough and I vowed to never let this ridiculous excuse of a mother win on any of her many attempts to tear down my innocence. I was still in there yearning to get out and enjoy life like all the rest of my siblings.

You know, these siblings would probably be shocked to find out that most probably a subject of so many investigations both on the private & on the Federal Level, although I having gone to college and took the right courses, know that the Southern form of Federal Raid will absolutely definitely be breaking all the rules simply due to the fact that I'm a proud member of the Chicano society, and no one and nobody can excise this fact out of me, nor will they ever succeed at making me feel ashamed of this fact as I was born and raised as a proud Mexican American which is the definition of us Shjicanos. So now I know how important it was to go to college to learn just how many ways that an American citizen can be violated! It makes no difference where I am, the voices are always the same, the sounds of mangy Red necks with their Southern accents always calling out "Mohican", why did he do that, well, "maybe they might think about the many ways I & or us Chicano's have been violated, and I will attempt to innumerate this in a later paragraph so my readers can begin to understand just why a person can break down when not by family, definitely by piers, such as classmates ostracizing you due to something as simple as your pigmentation or an accent that is different from theirs, whatever, there were so many ways that I was discriminated against in life, I'll have to probably dedicate an entire chapter to this "society's ill behavior".

A real important fact occurs to me right now as I'm writing these prophetically sad lines, & that is that the thing that probably makes me the maddest when I think of the way that I was treated over the years was that my potential has been overlooked & I'm almost sure that I truly would have way out done even my brother who works for the Govt. installation & the sister who has her masters degree in political science, or even my brother in law who has two doctorates degrees, but no, I was too effeminate, I was too dark, I didn't look European enough, but do I care about that, does anybody care about that anymore these days? Notwithstanding all of these put downs, and in spite of being drilled that I was never going to amount to anything, I decided after I had one breakdown too many, that I was going to pull myself up from my bootstraps one again, like I did so many times before, until this became a pattern with me, to start up with nothing and nobody giving me any encouragement but in the end, I would learn to turn to books as I was coming to the sorry awakening that the world or at least my world was going to have no mercy for me & I was only going to be regarded in such ways as a nuisance, a burden, I would be told constantly that I ate too much, there was no room for me, (one period, I would be made to live in a damp basement filled with black widows and there was nothing I could do about it because my mother had already had little sis Maggie, but I didn't want to sleep with my mom and dad anymore even though both parents made the offer, but I just felt that I already had pushed the envelope to have slept with them to the age of 11, but at least I hadn't hit puberty yet, at least give me that, & give my mom & dad that they wanted to be forever parents.

I'm the one who's been TO HELL AND BACK in more ways and more times that if it were you, than you would care to remember. In the South where I currently reside there exists what I consider the last throws of what Southerners consider their Great South, this Great Invisible Nation To their credit, these thugs have Raided virtually every property here in Florida that I own only to what I have heard them complain to lose their shirts, as some have put up their houses or some of their holdings. Hey, I only have to say, "you should investigate persons better than they have so that they do not take risks greater than their precious properties & or assets can handle. If this invisible Nation of hate is so potent, then why do I still own the majority of my properties that I always had & I enjoy interjecting also some of theirs, ha, ha! Could it be that this invisible nation bit off more than it could chew? Might it be that I decided to hurt anybody that had plans to hurt me? It so happens that right here where I live, the self proclaimed red necks are declaring that I'm still a fag, so pursuing my assets and tearing down anything I have built or plan to do is still part of their custom personal plan also to ensure that I accomplish nothing even including these lines I'm writing and plan to publish: arrangements have already been made for a linguist of no less than 5 languages (my son in law) to personally proofread for me and assist me in finding a proper publishing house. These conspiratorial types thugs from this South who generally live in ram shackled housing usually below standards actually claim that they run the south and their steak outs as I call these creeps that hold up in adjacent buildings also refer invariably to their selves totally unprofessional set ups (POLIT BUREAU's but I have also heard themselves refer to themselves as (Wolf's Lair's)) so what does that indicate & or tell you? Further, saying" "he's still a fag even though he has enabled himself to be able to protect himself" only reinforces my belief that due to the fact that Southerners dare not intimidate the "Blacks" that true to their self proclaiming edicts, they must go after Gays and Chicano's of which I proudly belong to both classes & I further declare to the world it's this Fag's edict to set up many more systems to protect & defend us minorities and Gays & also Lesbians by initiating a private fashion watch group and trust Fund to help persons being besieged by these hate groups the way I am being attacked and no matter how many time I either call the police or inform the FBI TIP line it's always to no avail so I am going to establish task force' and Trust Funds to carry out these lofty good deeds of truly protecting the new Niggers, as we're referred to by these criminal hoodlum types. The proceeds from this book will partly be dedicated to these ends. I can attest personally, that the Govt. here in Florida could care less whether I broke down or not, whether I'm being singled out by these hate groups, whether I'm writing about this or not, they just don't care about homosexuals at all period, & this Homo doesn't care whether they care or not too, but mark my words when the world hears about what has gone on with my life & what happened to me after I came here to Fl., I truly think that the police and the FBI TIP line will care then, & I hope some of these uncaring Fed. officials lose some of their jobs. These criminal hate cell's that are allowed in Florida also like to brag how they are evil, and this included raiding my properties, spreading ruthless vilifying gossip about gay people, stealing electric to the tune of about $2500.00 for about 7 or 8 months from my very own well that I kept running for the trailer park that I was in the process of shutting down, & the list goes on ad nauseum!

At the present time I'm being threatened by these thugs that I am going to be abducted and either be held hostage or for a ransom, ha, as if I had money, & believe me if this book generates any money of any kind I will be instituting these task forces as our Govt. doesn't give a flip about me or any other Gay's that complain as you see, the Govt. was set up primarily to protect the Families and precious hetero's who also have problems from time to time here in the most criminal state that I've ever lived in. If you ask me, these same hetero's who are asking for [unable to read] problems are some of the same ones who just 1 county from where I live here in a city in Fl. was allowed to publish a book instructing in detail on how to seduce minors down to the age of whatever you want even in the crib, and Now I ask, why isn't the Govt. going after these hetero creeps here in Florida?

This actually occurred in Polk Co. just one Co. over from where I am currently residing. Even further alarming is now we have a Republican governor who doesn't wish to have 2.4 Billion dollars to help Fl. build high speed rail, boy, "I hate to see what kind of money offers Fl. will be getting after I publish this book." If this state thinks that I'm going to let the Klan get away with what they claim already that they have gotten away with, by having gotten over on me with this stealing my electric, and raiding my trailer park while closing it down, they got another thing coming, I was told this by a charter Klan member who lived in my park and sure enough, it looks like this idiot carried these deeds out! I never put it past him, and the only reason he got away with this is because me and my buis. partner had moved out, so they could have a field day with what looked like a property that was being abandoned, but even though we have moved away, we required permission from anybody to take anything from that premises, "oh, but no, not from the possession is more percent of ownership mentality of these rag-tag southern types and their prostitutes, drug dealings, and theft/fence rings & etc. That's what the south has deteriorated to FOLKS, and you can believe it from a victim that experienced it 1st. handedly. God darned [unable to read] doesn't give 1 freaking flip about human rights for the Homo's, but they do like to court our vote but only to no avail.

Now let me describe if I can just how horrible these kinds of raids that I've been referring to are like as is my experience: 1st. of all, the 1st thing I hear when I wake up in the morning is these sleazy Southerner's voices piping in what they think of me as if I gave a flip the same way the Police down here do. the next thing they usually do is read my mind, or so they think they do, but they are definitely in a dilemma trying to do so, then I might get up to visit the bathroom so, the next thing that's done; "he's taking either a piss, or a ship, anyway, whatever it is I do, they recite it, then say something like, write it down, this dump is evaluated, something like, he didn't hardly do much or wow, he sure took a healthy one, so we better watch him extra close today, as I guess this implies that if One takes a healthy shit in the morning, they'll be much more be apt to be feeling their oats. What a bunch of blithering & drooling idiots these Creeps are to me! But there's much much more, than just monitoring your bodily functions, like also rating your sexual performance, or the quality of your or your lover's erection, I know even better than to rate my lover's erection quality! This guy even has to take Viagra & I also take an herbal version of Viagra.

The very sad truth of the matter in my case was basically cut and dried, a simple case of PTSD, TO THOSE WHO ARE SO stuck on hating gay people & would never be willing to accept that the torturing of a child because he or she were regarded as unacceptable whether for religious of social reason or not did happen! Why the hell else would a person with so much going for them go off the deep end with such terrible flashbacks of such criminal negligence and physical abuse many times not even experienced by our soldiers. For the functional illiterate thugs who prefer to encourage a breakdown by a gay person who is having such PTSD events I'll have to spell it out: PTSD stands for Post Traumatic Stress Disorder which our soldiers often experience after they have concluded their duty at war, & I emphasize that not only Gay people can experience this phenomenon, but also many of our sad American criminals also go through these horrific terrifying memory flashbacks the same way that our Heroic Soldiers do. may also go thru these kinds of events.

In my particular case, I was warned by a neighborhood that if I was having these events, this neighborhood would see to it that I would be slipped LSD, ecstasy, or some other kind of drug, so they said that this would then cause me to totally crack up, and then they could proceed to take away my rights to walk about freely & this would then enable these creepy neighbors to seize all of my assets, so they thought. I know for a fact that I was slipped ecstasy thru an herbal aphrodisiac at a corner Indian American operated local store, & I suspect that these conspiratorial creepy neighbors put these mean spirited Indians to place this on their displays so that I might buy this. I really must have been totally destructively out of my mind, as I had a suspicion that this was what was going on, however I just wanted to get high in hopes that I would forget my terrible flashbacks, but as these creepy conspiratorial neighborhoods work hand in hand, & I do remember this creep warning me about the fact that this kind of hoodwinks was going to happen!

Again, as I'm writing these lines they are also being read which gives me goosebumps, because I have no doubt that these same creeps that tampered with the (aphro) are also the same creeps that are reading these lines before they are published in the hopes that I'll never have a chance to publish these lines & this terrible story of Hoodwinks, sabotage, conspiracy, and back stabbing of a gay person simply because he bought into a neighborhood & into a region these people thought would always be in the (quote, un-quote) hands of the what they thought were superior white people & by the way also had to be heterosexuals. Further besides what I just mentioned, this neighborhood of what I considered idiots, these creeps told me that another part of their plan to defeat me was to locate an offended person so that these idiots could use for a patsy that would be crying that they were so offended that they wanted to be compensated but there has never been such an individual that has come forward I think because the offended person is definitely smarter than these creeps, additionally, these conspirators also declared that they had many criminal friends who would do their bidding for very little money, which would include many many raids on this tiny little trailer park that I and, my business partner were trying to make be a business for profit, not a welfare state, which was about what this entire neighborhood is to this day and from the looks of it when we bought this, it always has been due probably to the fact that there isn't anybody with any work worth mentioning, and virtually nobody has obtained any higher education practically without exception. These neighbors [unable to read] also had [unable to read] (heirs) argument so this was why they had more right they thought than myself or a Tyson. When I think about this it just makes me ant to spit bullets, because, when I attended the University that I went to, I literally had to hitch hike no less than 4 times to a 50 mile away Ivy League University that I had the privilege to attend but I really didn't have the wherewithal financially to finish this lofty goal I was attempting, but I sure wasn't going to miss my chance to take a final for my Perspective Law course for which I earned a B, at that time this made my day but later that day while hiking home, I nearly froze to death as a freak winter storm blizzard just suddenly came on & I thought I could make it home, but it got dark and this became a small blizzard & I barely made it to a farmers home who didn't want to let me in the door as I wasn't the right complexion, but I didn't want to die, so I forced my foot in the door and made my point, so they even agreed to take me to the neighboring town, but I had to give them gas money. To this day, I honor these people even though they didn't want to help at the start, they still got past their bigotry, and I even managed to get a smile from them, "you can attract more flies with honey than you can with vinegar!" I was actually almost unable to speak as my lips had become numb, but when I uttered this to the older woman who answered the door it didn't seem to flinch her, so sadly this was what I had to force my foot in the door because I saw in this woman's eyes a look of I don't know you or anything about you, so for all I know you could be a murderer! I just wanted to get home to my wife and children and studies that I was going to have to study for the next course!

As a final footnote with regards to the college farmers anecdote, as a result of my having been held in the cell beneath the brick school house, I for the rest of my life including now have been very susceptible to hypothermia, or I never would have bothered these farmers, as you know these farmers exploit Mexican American to tend to their crops and to harvest them, and they are the last people I also want to ask for help! This is one of the times that I as a result of destitute abject hopelessness I was forced to ask for help from the very type of people that I actually reviled, & yes I do and did still have my pride. Not 6 blocks from the very BGSU THAT I was attending, were tiny little shacks that may still be there cause you see, this town's main product is College Students & it is in the Midwest, and it is surrounded by farmland, wow, what a F'd up mess this appeared to me, still, I had to press on to be able to support a wife and 2 children, so I say to you, at least give me that even though I was a married homosexual, I knew that I had to be responsible enough to be able to have a trade to be able to provide well for them.

As I type these pitiful lines, I can hear these Raiders debating whether I'm worthy of raiding still, as my property is Pasco Co. Fl is barely hanging on by a thread & I have to wonder what does it take to make these crazy evil people go away, will I have to take their eradication into my own hands, & how could a little guy like me do that anyway? I'm not a powerful invisible nation of haters conspiring at every turn, I'm just one former disgruntled abused child that grew up and out of that terrible mess, but I have no way of stopping these people from destroying all that I've built up in that terrible neighborhood so, I have opted to just walk away and my only recourse is to write this book and exposé, and remember these raiders have always forewarned me that tearing down that which me and my business partner was what these people would be dedicated to.

These are some of these creeps statements: "all we have to do is call the law & they'll make him clean up the terrible little from tearing down the trailers, "We just have to tell his renters to not pay him, "we need to provide hookers so they won't have his rent, these low lives may also opt to attack my well from this formerly beautiful park and is now in ruins but this well is a vital water supply for this sole remaining house so since they know this esp. if they're reading these lines they will know that this is one of my weaknesses & I should interject that this neighborhood has already actually stolen the well that provided water to the house & to my disbelief these scoundrels have no limits, I definitely envision the oxycodone pusher planning to peddle his illegal prescription drug to my few tenants so that they would fall short on their rent. This treacherous neighborhood has many angles you see & I know for a fact that they conspire at every chance they can, they're always proclaiming their next moves either in my car, at my bungalow, or even if I go to the devastated former trailer park area, there's no escaping them, try as you might, & now I have my buis. partner convinced that this is what has been going on all along!

Thru no fault of my own now at the ripe old age of 43 the dreaded virus has got me, and I say this because I was practicing safe sex, I had a lover though I can't comment on this, but the point being that although I felt I would be immune from contracting this disease due to the above, this completely turned my world upside down! My lover had been warning that if I wasn't going to be faithful, even though we were having painful sex which was totally unsatisfactory to me, his warnings were that if I chose not to be faithful even in the light of this terrible sex that actually should have been beautiful the way it always had been, he would go and contract HIV and then give it to me so that I could never leave him. Well, I left this love some 10 years ago, (you can lead a horse to water, but you can't make him drink it.) Much was wrong with my sex life the least of this which was our discord, he also had a pedophile uncle move into the neighborhood who immediately started up with his lifestyle as thoroughly acceptable & he also wanted participation of this lover as well as my own. I felt that for me and my lover this was wrong but no matter how I protested, he would come over to visit & also would offer his siblings for sexual activities & I of course being ethical in this subject would always decline the offers & then would always include to this misguided uncle that I preferred to regard children as minors, illegal to do that with & about that time was when the painful sex with my lover began! If the painful sex didn't happen, then this now so called lover would squeeze very very hard at the moment of climax & make this hurt so much that it would take 2 or 3 days before the pain would go away! Too many things seemed fishy after this pedophile uncle came into the neighborhood but I knew the situation was totally out of control when this crazy so called lover would wait until I was ready to climax, & then he would bring up my son's name & lovingly interject that he and I would look good doing something like his uncle was suggesting, so I'd immediately ask him why the hell he dared to bring that up just before I would have the orgasm then I wouldn't, I'd lose my erection of course [unsure of word order], fly off the handle & tell him that if that was what he wanted was a sick lover that was a pedophile, he needed to start searching for one because, I would never be that way! Most of the times I got right out of the bedroom & never came back till the next day because this hurt me so much, I wasn't going to be needing this guy who was no longer a lover to me, but he was now a sexual abuser, & I wasn't about to assume the role of abused gay lover especially when I wasn't going to be sexually satisfied, & my changing my sexual ethics to please him and this misguided uncle. This neighborhood did plenty to destroy the threatening Fags, but then when they warned that they knew about this uncle & that they were going to encourage him to impose this on me, that was the worst thing that happened in my life to that point because up to that moment, I did have control of my and the lover of over 12 yrs. at that time's lives, and I know we had differences, but we were totally happy until this uncle moved by us and these creepy neighbors set out to psych. this very loved uncle of my lover's to figure out a way to separate our true love. How could I ever be expected to compete with teens any damned way anyway?

Suffice it to say that I have survived this the antics of a lover and an uncle who came into the neighborhood proclaiming the joys of being a pedophile, but obviously I didn't go along with any part of it. Now I suspect that the 7 or 8 yrs. I have been living with this new lover these Raiders have been continuously trying to sway this lover to also be attracted to younger love interests but somehow thru all of their barrage of constant put downs & suggestions that there's plenty out there that's much whiter, younger, without HIV, much more Detroit & the swinging lifestyle we're still together! This lover must still truly love me so I just might still have a little light at the end of that tunnel. If you are truly loved, then there's no talk of others except perhaps in entertaining a fantasy, and who of anybody that is still vital and quite sexual doesn't do that? That kind of banter doesn't bother me, but I even practice myself, but there's a big difference from the way we or I do this compared to the way the former lover was doing this! Family members of either of ours have never been brought up and certainly never just before the moment of the orgasm! I hate to have to write in this intimate manner, but the fact is although I was having terrible flashbacks of terrible childhood events, no matter how much I asked for psychological help & or intervention, none would be forthcoming, and instead, I got this from a lover and an uncle, and a horrific terrorist neighborhood that even touted to be KKK, Skinheads, Neo-Nazi, Arian Nation & even this uncle claimed to be a sympathizer of these hate I consider despicable invalid organizations.

This may be a rather radical departure from what I have been writing about but as I was talking about my childhood with my lover, a funny thing came, up, it was while Mack and I were talking about his having to wash his boxers by hand, "Mack, if you really want to hear about something gross and also typifying the older people it was something that my granny who was raising me would do regularly but she and I never talked about. Welita used to hang her 92 Yr. old woman's panties in our nasty bathroom after she had washed them because she was by the age of 92 slightly incontinent so these were almost always hanging above the shower stall, or if the weather was going to be dry and not too cold, she'd do us all the honor and hang them to dry outside along with her 19th century Victorian opaque style nylons with a thick line down the back like the olden days, what a beautiful welita I had that raised me with all of the love that any boy would have been more than satisfied to have been raised with!

Now, meantime let's see, now, back at the ranch these malfeasant neighbors who are always claiming they're real true Redneck Raiders, well, "they just said that it is up to them to destroy my immune system by inducing early (premature onset of full blown aids as they constantly brag that they know how to get to me so that they make sure that I get full blown fast, as in spike my foods & drink/intake, and I know they know where most of my food is obtained, thru Mack who works right next door from where both these creeps and we live, can you try to figure how the rest of this puzzle goes?

Of late I've been thinking a lot about the sadness of having to write about such a terrible life that I've had and how I ever was able to overcome so many adversities for instance, having to overcome being brought up in an extremely conservative religious neighborhood and an extremely conservative mother as well. The only remarks made or comments about homosexuality or being a member of such a group were pure put downs in the 50's and 60's when I was raised. Not only did I sustain bone cracking blows to the skull by a what I now realize was a mother who suffered bouts of psychosis (at these times she became very psychotic) and was capable of going off on anyone in the house and even my father might fear her! It was up to her, who it was that she was going to be picking out to take out her rage on. At such times, we would all share glances at one another, 5 scared, no terrified little children, a couple of us would literally be trembling and our foreheads would sweat from the prospect of being the one or ones chosen for some twisted game she might think up usually as one that would pit one against another & making only one be able to be the winner or champion as she would put it, included as a reward could be something twisted like not having to run around the house enough times until you can't anymore so that mom would make sure we would be tired out and then just have enough energy to fall asleep, ha, apparently this was her objective.

In this insidious village that allowed & even encouraged the abuse and even torture of a tiny little infant, but these villagers claimed that they were true Christians that also had NAZI parentage who instilled in them also to be proud of their German NAZI heritage although they had lost this war that they still should believe this NAZI theory & beliefs of this horrible regime just the same, and that included that they were superior, should feel just in having hated and killed Jews during WWII, and that any races other than the white race was inferior to the white race, Mexicans in particular were reviled by the NAZI's belief's, so, I, they would say to me was a dirty filthy Mexican in the eyes of these descendents of NAZI childhood peers that I was unfortunate to have to endure. At the same time that they said such things to me in my mind I was thinking of how I felt sorry for them because they looked so pale and to me sickly as a result of this sickly veins showing all thru this transparentish looking thinly looking skin, sometimes I'd often ask them if they had had enough to eat as I was sure these classmates must be sick to look to lifelessly white like a ghost or phantom to me, so I would counter with these sentiments to them only to have to have them burn my ears that I only said this because I was jealous which I can assure anyone that this was the sincerest truth being spoken by an uncorrupted pure mind. This innocence of mine was about to be corrupted by such filth, "In my child mind I still remember, I'm not going to let anyone that looks like that turn me against myself just because I don't look like that! When I might register this complaint to this sickening mother, she could counter with I'm white too like them but I can't do anything for you because you turned out too dark but I guess the only thing you can do is just ignore them which I had already figured this out. As sad and insufficient as this advice is from such an abusive mother, I guess I should give her the fact that she told me to just stay away from them, and yes to ignore them, but then that's when I began a life of loneliness as these child brother's and sister's got corrupted by these peers and were encouraged to think of themselves as white just like their peers so these little siblings learned from this school to shun their brother since he had gotten so dark from being cast outdoors to play in the beat down son & have little else to do but just wander about often aimlessly until someday sometime a friend might come along but I literally had to wait until my the 9th. grade before I really made 2 great friends that remained my friends until after I graduated. So thank God for that, else wise I might have become some kind of serial killer or something, but with these two true friends I learned once and for all the love of a brother like friendship, so thank you Mave and Meryl, for now these are their anonymous names. This might have been the only real well balanced period of my adolescence and I so valued these new found friends that they even tolerated my countering comments with regards to our differences in race and culture and language as I also had a tendency of being cocky and showoffy, but they knew it was all in fun. I had much pride due to my other brother's and sisters popularity & important posts in school, such as my brother being the star basketball and baseball star of all our school and was valedictorian and class president, 2 sisters that became cheerleaders, so this didn't hurt, to have these accomplished siblings for, kin, ha, ha. This shouldn't matter but at the time such things as your complexion getting lighter as you stop constantly being in the sun cause you to become Caucasian which I always was but I had this propensity to stay in the son & when I could reduce this because I was wanted suddenly, I then made the friends that this had managed to elude me most of my life, so now I from about 15yrs. old to 19 I'd enjoy a sense of fitting in and being a part of a community sort of but anyway for actually except for the closeness of my siblings, this was really my only indoctrination of any kind of social type from this brief 4 or 5 year period, that I can draw any kind of glue or adhesiveness to life & I really have to emphasize that were it not for this amazing sweet grandmother's love who gladly stepped up to raise the difficult I had become due to this mother terrible neglect and abuse, I have to emphasize my grann's touch saved me from a terrible fate that I might have ended up enduring were it not, for her constant never unavailable and enduring love & touch which I could get any time that I wanted & she made sure that I would as she would verbally remind me if I might tend to forget. This grandmother was smarter, than anyone gave her credit and now as I write these lines, I am moved to write that these are the real moments in my life and I think that much of the rest of it could qualify as surrealistic and nightmarish, yet I was always trying to win people over so that I might be liked, but now I see that all of those attempts of that kind were total wastes of time. Esp. Include But my granny wasn't a nightmarish surreal dilemma, I miss you wilita.

Why should I feel remorse in writing this book? Why should I feel ashamed to admit that I as a living being allowed someone else injure me that was supposed to be responsible for my well being? Why did a sister of this horrific mother have to blurt out when I least expected it that this absurdly sickening father of her's thoroughly enjoyed fiddling with this aunts clitoris? This aunt tended to drink so one time when I was visiting she had to be drunk & later I realized that she was because on several occasions I had been moved to stop her when she must have thought that I was willing to hear about such details & I remember distinctly on many occasions when we had been talking about our childhood suffrages that I would always say to her "please never tell me anything about this terrible background that you girls had suffered", much less to hear about her clitoris being mentioned. I myself was only trying to psychologically save some part of an upbringing, my thinking was that I could only think of these parent figures in a good light, perhaps I won't have these terrible events of their lives adding to my own anguish of what I had suffered. Were these terrible injuries incurred by my poor dear aunts and mother all performed by the same ill grandfather who I was told also so abused his wife in the form of terrible wife beatings.? The most terrible account by my mother and by the way her favorite one was by far the account of how my grandfather would like to brag to all the house of how his wife was just like a cave woman to him and he could drag her by the hair of the head just like the caveman he was, and so he would always do this when he would drink which would end up being literally whenever he wanted to or almost all the time.

My one sister also wanted me for some reason to know about all of these terrible things that our mother had endured/suffered/survived, but I as this already so neglected and so abused & criminally been tortured: also I was the youngest tenderest child I just saw this thru my mother as her ploy & also as a weak attempt to try and sway me away from any resentment towards this insufferable mother as if to excuse it away, but even as a small kid and as I became an adolescent I managed to fend off these attempts to tell me the facts of my own mother's sexual abuse and physical abuse, but I just knew that I had to hang on to some kind of sanity, normalcy, or cling to someone that could make feel like I'm connected to something that approached appearing normal, this would come to me in the form of a very dear and very aged grandmother who would live with us our entire life, so I felt very privileged and fortunate to have the good fortune of enjoying this wholesome experience with the most lovely Victorian grandmother anyone could ever hope for! I now viewed this mother as incomprehensible, one to run from, but still I was going to have to endure her trying to win me back, "yea, just so she could abuse and neglect again", no thank you, I'll pass!

FÍN